ROUGH ROAD

SCREAMING DEMONS MC
BOOK SIX

SUMMER COOPER
SIENNA CHANCE

LOVY BOOKS

"I'm going to kill you." It wasn't a joke. Fiona Strong-Owen meant it. She was going to kill him herself. Slowly. Kneecaps. Hands. Feet. Then if he was lucky, she'd put a bullet between his eyes. If luck wasn't with him or if he dared speak, she'd cut out his tongue, then his dick, then she'd kill him. The plan made her happy even as he tightened the rope around her wrists.

"Keep talking, little mama." He yanked the rope and Fiona fell forward onto the dirt floor. The whole place smelled like earth and dirt and old cigarettes. There was no furniture in what used to be a cabin and spider webs clung to every corner and the three windows.

London sat quietly in her carrier, oblivious to the grunge and danger. Thank God.

There were a hundred ways this could go and all of

them ended up with her dead leaving London in God knew what hands. Grier was her only chance. London's only hope. But she needed information. "What's the plan, here, Einstein?" Holding her hostage and not killing her immediately meant they wanted something. "Ransom, right? Or did they not tell you the plan?"

She memorized his face, the scar from the corner of his eye along his cheek and curved down from jaw to chin. Must've been one hell of a fight. His hair, a dirty blond, was cut short and tipped with white and spiked on top. And his eyes were the same color as a pile of shit. As a bonus, he smelled like he hadn't showered in the last year or so.

But none of that mattered right now. It would only matter if she got away and had to hunt this fucker down later. Right now, she needed to know what was in his head. His instructions. Maybe then she could figure their reason for holding her. Unless it was just the obvious—to cripple the Screaming Demons by asking for an unreasonable ransom or by… killing their leader. Of course, if that was the goal, why not just do it? Why bring her here?

The asshat didn't answer. "Seriously. You don't know." She rolled her eyes. "Great. How do I not rate someone in the upper ranks? Obviously, you're just one of the hired hands who does the dirty work. It's insulting, really." He cast a glance over his shoulder as he tied the rope to a pipe in what Fiona assumed was at one time a kitchen. And he was as dumb as a rock. All she had to do was slip the rope over the pipe.

He turned and smiled, his face reminiscent of something out of the old Batman comic books. "While you sit here and think about it, I'll just spend a little time— " he picked up the baby carrier, "— getting to know the kid. What do you think?"

Fiona swallowed hard. "Wait!" He dropped the carrier with a thunk and another sickening grin. The jolt of the seat against the ground startled the baby awake, and she scrunched her face then let loose a wail that could've meant pain. Fiona swallowed hard. "I'm sorry. I'll be quiet. Just don't take her."

He picked up the seat and walked closer to Fiona, but not close enough she could get to her daughter without crawling. "Shut her up or neither of you are going to last the night." Instead of walking out, he sat on the floor against the wall near the door, staring at her.

Fiona needed a plan of her own, a way to get past this buffoon without getting herself or her baby killed. But first, she had to calm London, hopefully let her daughter know she would kill or die to protect her.

"I need to feed her."

He shrugged. "So, feed her."

Fiona held up her bound hands. "I can't."

His smile made her stomach turn and she swallowed

back a mouthful of bile as he stood and crossed the room. More careful than she would have thought possible, he lifted London from her chair and handed her to Fiona who tried to maneuver the baby into position. London calmed and turned toward Fiona's still shirted breast. Dammit. She should've figured this out before. The baby fussed, and Fiona shifted to rest the baby across her lap as she unfastened the buttons to her blouse. The asshat cocked an eyebrow and stared. She met his gaze and lifted the cup of her bra.

"Never seen a boob before?" She rolled her eyes and slipped the rope behind the baby's back and lifted her so she could latch.

Asshat shook his head. "You're lucky I have orders not to touch you unless you get out of line." He stretched his legs out and crossed his ankles. "Did you *want* to get out of line?"

"Dream on." She narrowed her eyes and shot him a glare.

"You're high and mighty for somebody who's life is about to change in ways she's never imagined."

Sounded too much like a threat for Fiona's blood not to boil, but she tamped down the anger with a look at the baby. "Change how?"

He chuckled. "I think that's for us to know and you to fear."

"You don't scare me." Her voice was stronger than

she felt. She had no weapon, no plan for a way out, and no idea what the next few hours or days or weeks held.

He pushed to his feet and stalked across the floor to snatch the baby away from her. "Are you scared now?" He held London out in front of him, his hands curled under her arms. "What if I do this?" He spun in a fast circle and let London go only to catch her a second later. "We know your weak spot." He handed London back and Fiona's breath whooshed out.

But he'd told her enough. They wouldn't hurt the baby until they had what they wanted because Fiona was their bargaining chip, and the baby kept her in line. Now, she only had to figure out what they wanted.

GRIER FLOPPED over toward Fiona's pillow and breathed deep. Her perfume scented the pillow. Jesus, he wanted to feel her next to him, to run his fingers through all that shiny red hair, to hear her voice. But the danger here was too great, especially with Jez missing now. Plus, when he'd had Sage put her on the plane to Belize, he'd made her go without her cell. Didn't need Sedotal or Carr tracking her.

He sat up. Tracking her phone. The same way the Demons could track Jez's phone. Damn! Why hadn't he thought of that sooner?

The answer was simple. Finding out Jez was his mother was too new. Too fresh for his brain to focus on much more than that. He reached back for his own phone, dialed, and waited. "Come on, Sage. Answer the fucking phone."

It took another three or four rings before a groggy voice answered. "What?"

"Where are you? Can you get to a computer?" Urgency vibrated through him. Even though he hadn't known her as his mother for the entirety of his life, he knew Jez as a friend, as someone who'd helped him grow into the man he'd become by introducing him to Fiona's father, Max, the former leader of the Screaming Demons Motorcycle Club and Fiona's father. And now the club was in his hands while Fiona was away. Finding Jez wasn't just personal. It was club business.

"All right. I'm in front of the computer. What do you want?" Sage probably could have benefited from a couple of shots of coffee, but there wasn't time.

"I need you to track Jez's phone. If she has it with her, we'll use it to find her." She never went anywhere without her cell.

Seconds ticked off the clock while he waited. He shoved his arms through his shirt and pulled it over his head then smacked the phone back to his ear. The clicking of keys and the sound of Sage's breath only made Grier want his answer now. "Anything?" He pulled on his boots and stood to pace the floor at his side of the bed.

"A little harder than you might think. Hang on." The only problem with Sage, who Grier considered a friend now, was his normal laid-back demeanor. "All right. I have a location on the phone. I'll send it to you."

"I'll meet you at the clubhouse. Get the boys ready." Except for their personal pieces, the guns and ammo were kept locked up in a back room at the club. Grier hung up and went to the door. He looked back at the bed, thanking God he'd gotten Fiona out of there in time.

His head throbbed. Might have been lack of sleep, or it might have been the stress of the last couple of days—saying goodbye to Fiona and the baby, finding out his father was scum, finding out Jez was his mother and could have saved him from the childhood he'd endured —or maybe his stomach churned with anticipation. But tonight, he would put an end to all of it.

He blew through red lights, passed everything else daring to be on the road at one in the morning, and finally swerved down Hell Hollow road. Bikes lined up in front of the old steel factory that had been converted to the clubhouse years ago. Good. Everyone was there. He'd need them all.

Sage met him at the door. "She's at the compound."

Grier nodded. Of course she was. Back at the original scene of the very first crime. The former Screaming Demon compound where Max and Carr, Jez and a handful of others had started this club. "All right."

Grier walked beside him to the bar in the main room. "There's only one road in." They all knew it already from the surveillance they'd had on the groups of cabins and outbuildings. "And we're going in loud because we're also going in blind."

Sage was tough, a former Marine, who'd seen his share of battle and wore the scars as proudly as his tattoos, and when he frowned it meant something. But it wasn't his family on the line, his mother being held in the compound. Still, his opinion mattered. "What?"

"Let me take a couple of guys in through the woods. You need cover." Sage held up a rifle.

Grier nodded. "All right." They all knew who had the deadliest aim and she wasn't here right now, so Grier nodded to Hamilton, Weed, who had once been a cop— and Dirty Carl, a wild man who preferred axe to knife and old-fashioned bow to anything by Smith and Wesson or Glock, but damn he could blow the antennae off a butterfly at a thousand paces, too. "Enough?" Grier turned to Sage almost regretting his quick agreement. He needed all the firepower he could get his hands on at his back.

"Yeah. We'll leave you the entrance side and we'll come in north, south and west." Sage jabbed his finger into the bar once for each word as if there was a map there. Probably was. But only in his own head. "Ham can cover the east as you come in."

Grier finished the plan, handing out assignments, waiting for the adrenaline to kick in. His gut told him they were riding into an ambush, but what choice did he have. Jez was as much a Demon as any of them and no Demon life was expendable.

And now it was time to go save his mother.

2

Fiona wrapped the baby in her blanket to ward off the chilly air blowing through the holes in the walls and the broken window. A thousand smells assaulted her nose, not the least of which was the diaper she'd just changed with her hands still tied. Oh, the skills she'd acquired. Grier would be so proud. Aside from the diaper, she smelled ocean—fishy, salty ocean. And she could hear the squawks of seagulls.

The asshat still sat against the door. He hadn't spoken anymore, nor had he stopped staring at her. He watched her feed the baby, change the baby, lean back against her own piece of wall and hold her baby. It would have unsettled her had she not been so busy trying to figure a way out of here. "I'm hungry."

"You'll get food when I say so."

She chuckled as if she had something to laugh about.

"What you mean is, they haven't given you permission to go get food yet, because we both know the value of the commodity you have sitting in front of you. And whoever you work for needs me alive, so that means I get food. You just aren't allowed to decide when."

His eyes flashed and narrowed as his face brightened into a deep plummy red. So, she continued. "Errand boy, right? Got the shitty little job of watch but don't touch." She clicked her tongue against her teeth. "So… which is it? You piss off the big guy or do you just suck so bad they give you all the shit jobs?"

"Shut up, Fiona."

She shrugged. "I don't care one way or the other. Although, like I said, it's a little insulting for someone like me… important enough to be kidnapped and held, to be supervised by someone so low on the totem pole."

This time he laughed. Threw his head back and made sounds that reminded Fiona of hyenas or maybe a donkey's bray. "Stupid, bitch. It isn't about you. It's your boy we want. And once we get him, we're going to kill the three of you." His smile died. "I'm going to make him stand right over there—" he pointed to the corner, "—and watch me fuck you before I take my knife and slit you from pussy to eyeball." He chuckled. "I heard you like it rough and that's my specialty. I'm gonna make you beg for me just like you beg him."

Fiona's mind spun. She didn't care about the threats.

Well, she did, but the more she talked to this asshat, the more details he revealed. He was someone who'd seen the videos taken in her house. She didn't know for sure, but she would've bet all her money on it. Someone connected to Tyler Sedotal.

"So, what'd you do to piss Tyler off?"

He jerked his head toward her. "What?"

And she had him. Tyler Sedotal was behind this. Probably revenge for the gunshot. Although that didn't mesh with their wanting Grier. "What did you do? Screw his woman?"

"You're gonna be his woman."

"Thought you said I was gonna be dead. Was that just talk to make you feel better about yourself?" She laughed at him and his skin darkened to a deep shade of purple.

"I haven't decided yet."

She rolled her eyes, dramatically. "Oh, come on. We both know you don't get to decide anything. You're just some expendable piece of shit. He knows, and I know, and you know that if I wasn't tied up right now, you'd be on the ground with the heel of my boot sticking out of your throat. Untie me. Let's see." He didn't move and with each word, she felt braver. "Oh, I get it. You need me tied up so you can live out your pathetic little rape fantasy. Because we both know you aren't getting a woman without rope and chloroform and that gun on your hip." She laughed again, and he lunged forward to backhand her.

The coppery taste of blood meant he'd split her lip and goddammit, she couldn't fight back while holding her baby. She sniffed and swiped her tongue over her lip. He was gonna pay for that one. "I'm gonna like taking that hand."

He sat on his heels and brushed her hair back from her face. "I'm gonna like seeing you try."

If he leaned in to kiss her, she would throw up, empty stomach or not. And that breath… Dear God. She had to get out of here soon.

Asshat moved back to his side of the room by the door. "Maybe I'll just tell Tyler you put your hands on his woman." The words tasted like hell, but her smile didn't falter.

He laughed again. "Oh, don't worry, honey. Once you get your brand, we all get a shot before you graduate to Ty. He likes his women broken and broken in."

The thought turned Fiona's stomach. "But not until he says so, right?" He looked away and Fiona knew he'd crossed a line he shouldn't have. "Where are we, anyway?" He turned to her and shook his head. She tried again. "Honestly, who am I gonna tell? I don't have a phone and I'm tied to a pipe."

"Florida. Had to go on a little run. Don't get comfortable."

Oh, yeah. Not much chance of that while she was sitting on a dirt floor with a growling stomach and a bladder about to burst. "I need to use the bathroom."

He shrugged and motioned to a bucket in the corner. "So, go."

Fuck. She was supposed to be in Belize, sunning herself on a beach on Kye's private island and instead she was stuck with asshat in a rundown cabin in Florida with a bucket to piss in. And a broken window to throw it out of. Good thing she wasn't hysterical, no matter what her urge to sob said.

But the bucket was closer to the pipe and if she could manage to get the rope over the top without this stupid fuck noticing, she had a chance.

* * *

GRIER'S BIKE roared up the road, man and machine streaking through the night with a purpose. Saving Jez. Finding Sedotal or Carr or both. The night was cold, stark, and his gut churned with anticipation. Hopefully, they could end this shit tonight, and he could bring Fiona home.

He made the turn onto the road that led to the compound. Sage had left with Hamilton and the others in plenty of time to be in place, but there wouldn't be a signal, nothing to tell him whether or not they were walking into an ambush. He pushed his bike until the motor screamed and the wind bit at his face until he skidded to a stop in front of the first cabin. He jumped off the bike and leaped onto the small porch to burst through the door.

There were seven cabins and three outbuildings in various states of disrepair, but there was also some sort of tunnel system underneath that led to another entrance to the compound. Grier walked out to the porch of the last cabin to find the rest of the club assembled. "We need to check the tunnel."

And once bitten, Grier wasn't willing to risk the whole club. Clearly, the Omens had deserted the compound, same as when they left the stolen Demon merchandise unguarded but lined the crates with explosives that blew up as Grier led the way from the compound. He'd lost Demon lives once. He wouldn't be doing it again.

He would have preferred taking Kye below ground with him, and Sage was still in the woods, so he motioned to One-eye and Diamond Dave. He wanted to tell everyone to stay sharp, to shoot anything that moved and wasn't wearing Demon colors, but his throat closed, and his gut tightened. He nodded instead and checked his gun. Loaded. Ready. And he'd go in first.

One-eye followed Grier down the small ladder and though he'd looked down the hatch from one of the cabins, Grier hadn't made it to the lower level when they'd found the compound or when they came to collect their stolen goods, so he'd not seen the intricacies of the tunnels. The walls were reinforced with steel beams and rods and the ceiling was supported by steel with wooden planks. Where Grier thought they would have to hunch or duck, he stood tall, moved silently against the walls. Every hundred or so yards, another ladder led to another hatch. Where the tunnel itself was a long hallway with wires attached to lights that no longer worked thanks to the lack of electricity. It reminded him of a mineshaft he'd seen in an old movie.

Grier edged forward, a flashlight in one hand, his gun in the other.

The walls dead-ended at a door, a door secured by a combination pad with metal buttons that clicked when he pushed them. It beeped when he chose the wrong numbers. He aimed his gun at the little keypad and Diamond Dave put a hand on his arm. "Grier, don't shoot it. You'll short it out, and we might never get it open."

Maybe but… "How the fuck are we supposed to figure out the combination?"

One-eye moved from behind the shadow of Diamond Dave's body. "Long shot but try 2-2-5-6-9." When Grier stared at him, Dave shrugged. "It's her birthday. I'll explain later." When neither Grier nor Dave moved more than to stare at him, he motioned his flashlight toward the box. "Let's see if it works."

Grier punched in the numbers and the door clicked then popped away from the frame. Dave pried it the rest of the way and Grier walked inside with Jim at his back. The walls and floor were white, pristine. Hell, they could've done surgery in here. The room was wider than the hallway but empty, and Jim walked to a door on the other side. No keypad this time, just a knob he turned and walked through while Grier and Dave didn't move. This could be a trap, and no way was he getting too far from that door. Not when the only light he had was a flashlight and his gun would hardly be a match for a door three inches thick and something right out of a bank vault.

"Shit." Jim's voice carried through the door and echoed in the small room a second before he returned.

Grier shined the light on his face. Jim, always pale and in need of some serious time in the sun, was worse than normal, almost transparent even in the semi-darkness. "What?" Grier moved to the opposite door, that ball in the pit of his stomach, bigger and harder to ignore.

Jim grabbed his shoulder. "Don't go in there. You should just get out of here and let me take care of it."

And now he had to know what was on the other side. His heart thumped loud enough he thought they would hear it, but still he walked through, shined the light on the floor. "Oh, God." Blood. And Jez. "Aw, fuck." His shoulders shook as he lifted her head and cradled it against him. "Oh, God." The sobs came, for the friend he'd lost and the mother he never really knew. "Oh, God."

She'd been beaten, stabbed, murdered, probably scared and alone when the life drained out of her. "Fuck." It took a minute and some muscle, but he lifted her and carried her out, down the hallway to where they'd come in. Jim and Dave followed. He put her over his shoulder and struggled up the nine rungs of the ladder, but he couldn't leave her down there. Not when it was his fault she'd been killed, when he hadn't protected her, when he'd let her die alone or in a room with the bastards who should have taken him instead.

Grier didn't feel anything except the ache of every bone and muscle, the burning in every cell. If he let the emotion back in, he would curl into a ball and surrender. He concentrated on the physical pain and laid Jez on the floor in the cabin and knelt beside her, holding her hand now. The damage he hadn't seen in the tunnel he could now see in shocking vividness, and it stole his breath, tore at his gut. The odd shape of her face, the knife wounds, the dislocation of her knee and several fingers. They hadn't just killed her. They'd tortured her. And now, the Screaming Demons were going to return the favor. If he accomplished nothing else in his life, he would avenge Jez. He leaned down and pressed a kiss to her forehead. "I promise. I will get them."

When he caught his breath, he brought her outside, looked at One-eye Jim, Diamond Dave and each man who stood watching him. "Burn it down."

3

Fiona watched the asshat sleep. His mouth hung open and a slim line of drool inched down his chin. Disgusting. Plus, the bastard hadn't moved away from his post guarding the door and trying to get past him would be near impossible, but she couldn't just sit here and wait for whatever was supposed to happen next. She had to get the baby to safety then figure out how to call Grier. She scooted toward the pipe where he'd tied the rope. If she could get it off of there and… he shifted, and she sat straight, only a few inches closer than she had been.

Another few feet and she'd have it. Her heart punched her ribs and her stomach flipped and flopped with what she would never admit to being fear. She swallowed a gulp of air and looked down at the baby across her lap as she edged closer to the pipe. Since asshat had tied a knot Houdini couldn't undo, she would have to do all of this, untie the rope, make it to her feet and run with the baby held as tightly as her binding would allow, but damned if she could see another way.

She moved the last few feet and slid the rope over the pipe, never taking her eyes off the buffoon by the door. Wiggling and writhing, she made it to her feet with London against her chest. Her heels were quiet against the dirt floor, but no way could she run with the baby in her arms and her balance off-kilter thanks to her bindings. Of course, no telling what was outside this damned cabin. Forest? Beach? She had no idea and kept the shoes on.

Now or never. She tiptoed to the door and took a long breath. Asshat had turned his head to his opposite shoulder, so as long as she was careful, and London stayed sleeping there was a fair chance, probably her only one, that she could get out of the door without him waking her up. She twisted the knob and pulled. Nice and slow. A small scrap of wood against dirt and freedom.

"Well, hello, Princess. Leaving so soon?" Tyler Sedotal towered over her in the doorway and Fiona's guts dropped. She should've known.

"Thought I'd get some fresh air. Your watchdog kind of stinks."

Tyler threw his head back and laughed then cocked

an eyebrow. "But we have so much to talk about. So much to do." He took a step forward and Fiona took one back. "Calls to make. Husbands to lure." His eyes narrowed but his sick smile never wavered. She moved his name up a few spots on her mental list of people to kill. "I would have been here sooner, but I had some business to take care of back in Pine Hill."

Two more men walked in behind him and asshat stood in the cluster of stupid fucks who thought she was nothing but a little woman who couldn't defend herself. This time, she would show him, show them all. But first, she needed to know something, the wheres and whys. She turned to go back to her spot, the end of the rope still in her hand so Tyler or one of his goons couldn't grab it. While it wasn't much, it was the only weapon she had, one they could just as well use against her.

She laid the baby in her seat and remained standing. Sedotal crossed to her and yanked her against his chest. "We are going to have some fun, you and me."

"Why are you doing this? The Demons are going to kill you." That wasn't quite true. She was going to kill him. But not yet.

He laughed again and she caught a whiff of whiskey and cigarettes. "You think so? Because once I take their money and their action, I think the pendulum is gonna start swinging my way."

"Pendulum? Big word."

He yanked her head back with a handful of hair and put his mouth against her ear. "I've always admired your spirit. I can't wait to break it."

Yeah. She needed him to underestimate her. It would make him let his guard down. Or no way would she have let herself look afraid, would never have widened her eyes and chewed her lip. And damned sure that whimper wasn't a sound she ever made. For now, until she could see a way out, she'd give him what he wanted.

He shoved and she hit the wall behind her. For that, she'd take an eye. It would've made more sense to take the hand, but she didn't like the way he looked at her any more than she liked the way he pushed her. Oh, what the hell. She'd take the eye and the hand. But she kept it to herself as he pulled a phone out of his pocket and checked the time. "We have a couple of hours before we have to make a very important call, so come, sit. Let's have a talk, shall we?"

He grabbed ahold of the rope and jerked so that she landed on her knees in front of him. She considered using her head as a weapon since she was just about at the right height to drop him, but there were three of his cronies in the cabin, and she didn't have a plan for them. Yet.

He pulled her head and tilted his hips toward her.

"Anxious. I like it." To her credit, she didn't vomit at the thought. Instead, she went with her scared look again. "You're not so tough, are you?"

"Why are you doing this?" She even made her voice weak.

"Because I can. Because once I deliver the goods, he'll let me kill your man." He winked and sat across from where she still knelt in front of him. "Now, let's talk."

* * *

GRIER STARED down into his glass. Still numb. Still holding it together enough to sit upright. That was something, at least. The clubhouse was silent. No chatter. No banter. No TV in the background. They'd toasted Jez then slipped silently into grief. She'd been theirs, a part of the very essence of the Demons and her absence—he couldn't bring himself to say death—wasn't something any of them knew how to handle.

He sat between One-eye and Sage unable to speak or think. Right now, all he could do was thank God he'd gotten Fiona out of there. That she was safe with Kye. If he lost Fiona, on top of everything else, he wouldn't survive. Even if every day of his life had been a picnic filled with happiness and joy, losing Fiona would kill him.

His phone vibrated across the counter and he only

looked at the screen because he thought it could be her. When Kye's name and number appeared, he breathed a sigh. He would have to tell her. And she'd want to come home. Stir the boys into action. Get results. Which was what he should've been doing, but he didn't have quite the heart for it yet. But God he wanted to hear her voice.

"Hey, babe."

Instead of Fiona, Kye answered. "Hi, honey."

Maybe if he practiced on Kye… "Jez is—" his voice cracked, and he closed his eyes, "dead."

"Oh, God, man. I'm so sorry. What happened?"

Grier gave him the bare facts - the compound, the stolen stuff, the rival gang. He left out the condition of Jez's body, that she was more to him than just a Hell Kat at the club who'd saved his life.

"Oh man. Goddamn."

Grier nodded. "Yeah."

"I wondered why Fiona never showed."

"Yeah." He'd answered automatically and it took a second before the words registered. "What?" He shoved his barstool back and stood, bracing his free hand against the bar. Fiona was supposed to be with Kye, safe and sound on a secluded island. If she wasn't… "Sage put her on a plane last night."

"No planes in since yesterday afternoon. I've been at the airstrip all day."

When the feelings came, they came as rage, a fury so

powerful his grief evaporated, and Grier yelled and threw his glass of whiskey at the wall. "Fuck!" The glass exploded and the silence of a moment ago shattered with it. Chairs moved. Men stood. Glasses clanged against the table. And Grier tuned it all out to focus on the news he'd just received. "Fiona isn't with you?"

"No. She never showed."

Grier dropped the phone and grabbed Sage by the front of the shirt and slammed his back against the bar. "Where the hell is she? I trusted you with her!"

"I put her on the plane, Grier. Last night. I saw the flight plan myself. One stop in Florida then straight to Belize." Grier jerked him forward then back again. "Fuck, Grier!"

A crowd gathered but no one moved. "I'll fucking kill you!" He clenched one hand into Sage's shirt and drew back the other. The punch landed between Sage's jaw and cheekbone and spun his head sideways. As Grier was about to strike the second time, Hamilton grabbed his arm. He let go of Sage's shirt. "Nobody knew but you and me. I sure as fuck didn't tell." He turned then whirled back. "You better pray to whatever fucking God you believe in that nothing happens to her or my baby. Or I'll make your death so slow… so painful… you'll wish you never met any of us, you son of a bitch."

Sage slouched against the bar but looked over his shoulder at the bartender who had begun to move toward the side door. Grier had seen her once or twice, with Sage, that he remembered but didn't know her name. He pointed at her. "Stop. You." She folded her hands on the bar top then to her sides. It had to be fear that made her jittery and unable to look at him. And damned if he cared. If Sage had had any part in hurting Fiona, Grier would kill the girl, too. "Who are you?"

"Mia." She hid behind the veil of her long hair. "Mia Giovanni." She had long, black hair and brown eyes that couldn't hide her fear.

Sage stood to his full height which put him almost nose to nose with Grier. "Leave her out of it, Grier." A pretty ominous warning for a guy Grier had already decided a traitor who put his wife and baby into enemy hands.

Sage showed his hand too soon. He liked this girl and until Fiona reappeared safe and sound with their baby, Sage would suffer in any way Grier could make possible. Starting with his whore. He looked at Hamilton. "Hold him." He walked behind the bar, pulled a knife from his boot, and grabbed the girl. Nothing was out of bounds until he had Fiona in his arms again. He dragged Mia to the front, where everyone would see, but more importantly where Sage could see. "Where's Fiona, Sage?"

Sage stared at him. "Don't do this, Grier. I don't know. I put her on the plane."

Grier moved the knife an inch and a trickle of blood ran down the girl's throat. "Where is she?"

"I don't know." Sage struggled against Hamilton and threw his head back into Hamilton's throat, but the big guy didn't even flinch. Grier didn't move the knife this time. Instead, he jerked the girl, and she cried out. He wouldn't slit her throat until he had to. But if he had to, she wouldn't go alone. "Stop. Grier, Fuck!" He jerked and struggled, but Hamilton held tight.

"Tell me where my family is."

"Grier, it's me. You know I wouldn't do anything to hurt you or Fiona."

Bull shit. It had to be Sage. "Then how the fuck did they know?"

He'd thought Sage was a friend. Another mistake in a long list of them. And this time, this betrayal cost too much, might have even cost Jez her life. But he couldn't murder the girl. Sage, though, was a different matter.

But Grier needed to think before he did it. He'd had blood on his hands before, but never a brother's. And damned if he'd ever killed a woman. He shoved her away. "Take them to the cells and stay with them." He looked at Hamilton. If ever that man was an ally, it was right now. Fiona was his friend as much as his leader. And the cells below the club where Hamilton had thrown him not so long ago would do to keep Sage from spilling Demon secrets to whoever he'd been spying for, although Grier had a pretty good idea. "If he says anything other than where Fiona is, cut *her* tongue out."

First Jez and now Fiona and London. The only thing Grier knew for certain was that this was personal, not an attack on the Demons but on him.

4

Fiona sat across from Sedotal watching him. The man had no tells, nothing that gave away more of his plan than the few bits he'd told her, to take the money and the business her father had built. He didn't mention Grier anymore than he had in those first few minutes.

He stretched his leg and winced. "Yeah, a leftover from our encounter in your apartment."

"Sorry." Not really. He'd come there hoping to rape her. That she'd shot his leg and not where she'd hoped meant she needed to work on her hand to hand aim. Not a mistake she would make a second time.

"A couple of inches to the left and we'd be having a very different conversation."

A couple of inches to the left and she wouldn't have to worry about the way he was leering at her. She stayed quiet because telling him she would've preferred to change his gender wouldn't enhance her overall safety. Her ass ached from sitting so long on the floor listening to him babble about his plans for her club, and she would have sold her soul for a change of clothes and a piece of Jez's homemade meatloaf. "I don't suppose anybody thought to grab my suitcase from the plane."

He leaned back on his hand and cocked his head. "I have it." His gaze traveled the length of her body and she wanted to curl into herself, shield as much as she could, but she remained still until he smiled. "So, tell me. What's in Belize for a motorcycle club princess?"

Well, for his information, she was a motorcycle club queen, but she shrugged. "A friend."

"Not your friend, though. *His* friend."

"Why such a hard-on for Grier?"

Tyler shook his head. "You were supposed to kill him when he came back, not let him make you his bitch." He cocked an eyebrow. "You let me down, Fiona. I watched. I waited. I listened and yet that bastard got to walk into your house, put a kid in you, got your guys blown up. And still, you're the loving, doting, sucking his dick wife."

If he thought any of those things would do more than make her angry enough to add to the amount of time she took killing him, he was going to be sorely disappointed. She smiled because he wasn't the only one with a poker face. "None of those things affected you."

He chuckled. "Oh, but they did." He paused and twisted his mouth into a scowl. "In ways you can't even imagine."

"Tell me."

He sighed, bent his leg and let his hand dangle over it. "You know who my dad is?" When Fiona nodded, he continued. "And his mom."

"Mm-hmm."

He rubbed his free hand up and down his chin. "So dear old dad has never even met our boy, Grier. But he put out the word that Grier isn't touchable. Then he busted me down after I blew up a truck that didn't hurt more than your family business."

Hmm. Interesting. "Why does he care about Grier?"

"Right?" Tyler shook his head. "He's nuts. Thinks somehow he's going to get that Demon whore back and you'll all be some big happy family. He'll have a grand-kid, his woman, Grier will get a spot in the club. My spot." His poker face faded into a smile, one as evil and malicious as Fiona imagined he could form. This time it worried her. She hadn't climbed into scared yet, but she was closing in at warp speed. "She isn't coming back."

"What does that mean?"

"It means… nothing that makes a difference to you."

Even his laugh sounded evil. "Unless you liked the idea of a mother-in-law."

Oh, God. Jez. Fiona swallowed hard. She couldn't stop herself. Her stomach churned. And it could have been hunger, she would have been happy to call it that, but it was more about Jez.

"Let's just say, I saved you a lot of awkward holidays." His smile so smug, his voice so proud, and Fiona wanted to choke him until his eyes bulged and he slumped his way into hell.

If he hurt Jez, she would repay him in ways that drew out his death, in ways that assured suffering. Over a period of days. Maybe even weeks.

She wanted to clutch her stomach, will the pain away, but she sat straight, one arm absently rocking the baby chair, the other tapping a beat on her jeans. "This is all your fault, you know. You and that fucking father of yours. If you'd just left him where he was, none of this would have ever happened. We would've stayed under the radar, left you alone. You brought this on. Just you."

That was rich and she wanted to roll her eyes. She shrugged instead. "I didn't have all the information."

He scooted closer and ran a finger over her forehead then down her cheek. She didn't recoil, but it took every ounce of will she had. "All those losses… our men, your money, your fault and all you can say is you didn't have the information." He slapped her cheek. "I expected better. Did having the kid make you weak?" He turned from her to the car seat and twisted it to face him. He unsnapped the straps and lifted London, held her up, and stared at her. After a moment, he cuddled the baby to his chest. "Uncle Tyler." His mouth twitched and Fiona thought he might smile. Instead, he scowled at her. "You think I'm such a bad guy, but I hate collateral damage. Like the whore. The kid. But don't worry. Once I merge the clubs and we rule the whole city, I'll give you another baby. You won't miss this one."

Oh, God. Fiona's head spun. "Please don't hurt her. I'll do whatever you want." What choice did she have? Until she could figure out what to do… until she could get out of there…

"Yeah, but I can't have *his* kid around." He clicked his tongue and stroked the fine tuft of hair that laid over the soft spot where London's skull hadn't fused. Oh, God. She just wanted her baby back. "She's cute. Looks like you." He sighed and laid London in her chair more gently than Fiona expected and she almost thanked him. But he spoke first. "I've never hurt a kid before."

She swallowed hard and moved close enough to lay her still tied hands on his chest. "You don't have to now. I'll do whatever you want. I'll give you everything I have. The club, the money… everything."

He nodded but laid his arm over her shoulder and

leaned his forehead against hers. "That was never your choice."

She had to think. Fast. Save her baby. Save herself. "I know but do you know what would hurt Grier more than killing London? What would destroy him?" She blinked and pulled back so she could see more than his eyes and nose. "Knowing he lost us to you. Seeing it every day. Knowing I chose you over him."

"Do you choose me, Fiona?" There was a challenge in his voice that meant she might not have gotten through, but she'd at least, made him think.

"If it saves my baby? You bet I do." Of course, she would never stop trying to get away.

He nodded then turned to the asshat at the door and nodded. Asshat stood and went outside then returned with a long piece of steel rebar welded to another owl-shaped piece. A branding iron. Oh, fuck.

GRIER STARED at the computer screen, watching Sage and Mia Giovanni stand at the bars between them, his hand laid over hers. "I told you I would protect you, but you have to tell him."

Grier twisted the volume knob on the speakers. Definitely worth listening to, even if Hamilton stood over him, literally breathing down his neck as they watched the surveillance inside the cells.

"He'll kill me."

"He won't if you help him find Fiona. That's all he cares about right now." Sage reached through the bars and tucked Mia's long, black hair behind her ear. "I will do everything I can to keep you safe."

She scoffed and Grier admired her spunk. "In case you haven't noticed, genius, you're behind your own set of bars."

"He knows I would never hurt him or Fiona. He's just hurt over Jez and in shock. His mind has too much stuff going on to wade through it all. When he calms down, he'll know I didn't sell him out."

"But he'll know I did."

"That's why you have to tell him yourself before he finds out on his own. You have to be the one."

She turned away from the bars and faced the opposite wall. All the other cells were three concrete walls with a barred door. These two, with a wall of bars between them and concrete on either side, Max had built with the intention of listening in on conversations. Although, as far as Grier knew, he'd never really used the cells, preferring an immediate death sentence to making his subjects wait in the cells. Of course, he knew none of this from Max or Fiona, but from Hamilton.

"What do you want to do?" Hamilton stood and braced both hands on the back of Fiona's chair.

"Bring her here. Bring them both." Without Fiona, without the confidence she gave him, Grier didn't know what to do, and if Max had taught him anything, it was to end a small problem before it became a big one.

He pulled the gun from his waistband and checked the magazine. The sound of the mag slipping into place and the click of the slide comforted him. But damned if he wanted to shoot Sage. Of course, he would if he had to. For Fiona. For London. For Jez. And Mia, he decided, was already as good as dead.

He put the gun on the desk and waited for the door to open, for Hamilton to shove them through then shut them in, standing guard in case they went squirrely and tried to run. He gave Hamilton a slight nod of thanks then turned to Sage. "Sit down and shut up. Understand?" Sage sat but gave no further indication he cared. Grier looked at Mia until she shifted from one foot to the other. "Who are you?"

"Mia Giovanni." Her voice was small. "I was sent here by…" She swallowed hard and looked down then back up at Grier. "I was sent here by Tyler Sedotal."

"Why?"

"He wanted someone on the inside besides Kale."

Grier glanced at Hamilton wishing, not for the first

time, that he was Fiona. He blew out a breath and glanced at Sage. "You know?"

"Not all of it."

Grier had never been much for spotting the lie. And he wanted to believe Sage. He stood and walked around the desk to lean a hip on the front. "What did you tell Sedotal?"

She didn't look away. "That Fiona was going to be on a flight out. I didn't know when or where from, but I gave him the number of the guy Sage called to arrange it." She shifted again and a tear slipped down her cheek.

Grier nodded, each breath a struggle. "How did you get that information?"

She glanced over her shoulder at Sage and he nodded. "I waited until he was in the shower then I went into his phone. He had nothing to do with it." Sage didn't move. He continued to stare at Grier as Grier stared at Mia. "I might know where she is."

Grier cocked his head, but didn't speak, couldn't have if he tried.

Hamilton moved away from his spot by the door and came around to stand beside Sage's chair. "Where?"

"He has a fishing shack in the Fort Lauderdale." Florida? "I went there once with him.

It's secluded and I think that's where he would've probably taken her."

"Do you know how to get there?" Again, Hamilton spoke when Grier remained silent.

She shook her head and all of Grier's hopes faded. "I don't."

Then she'd already outlived her usefulness. He only had one more question. "Did you tell them about Jez? Where she lived? Where to find her?" Okay. Three questions.

"No. He already knew about her. When he was here… they… had a night."

Grier's stomach turned and bile rose up from his gut to his throat. That bastard had probably told Mia to make sure Grier knew it, too. "You know all the family history?" She nodded and tears, an entire batch, slid down her cheeks to wet her shirt as they dropped off her jaw and chin. It didn't matter. He still wanted to kill her. "And you thought I needed to know that?"

Sage stood as Grier advanced. He pulled Mia behind him, using his body to shield her. "You asked her, Grier. It's not her fault if you don't like the answer."

Grier reached for the gun on the desk. He pressed the barrel against Sage's forehead. "Move."

Sage shook his head, the gun moving with him. "No. If you're gonna kill her, you're going to have to kill me."

Grier didn't give a fuck. He wanted his wife back and his baby. Sage and the woman behind him didn't matter anymore.

5

If anyone ever doubted her grit again, Fiona would happily kill them. She now had a brand, a burn in the shape of an owl, on the side of her throat and for good measure, Tyler had put another on the inside of her thigh, his initials. The bastard had no idea the punishment she sat planning for him despite his praise. "You're pretty ballsy. Ryder passed out when he got his brand."

She'd take ballsy. And she'd cram it up his ass first chance she got. But for now, she had a game to play. "So, what's next?"

He pulled out his phone, his smile enough to make her vomit in her own lap. But she held it back as he considered her with his head cocked and his eyes narrowed. "Now, we make a call and see just who's more important to you."

"I'm calling Grier?"

"No. The big guy." He meant Hamilton. *Big guy*, no matter who said it, always meant Hamilton. "I gotta get him out of the way so I get a clear shot at your husband."

She smiled and ran her hand down his chest. She could feel corded muscle and probably a scar, some raised line across his chest. With a long breath, mostly to settle her stomach, she twisted the collar of his T-shirt around her finger and tugged him closer to rub her nose against his. "My ex-husband."

He grinned back and brought her hand to his lips, sucked her index finger into his mouth then handed her the phone as she swallowed back a mouth full of vomit. "You make the call and then we gotta get on the road."

She dialed Grier's number hoping he wouldn't know it. Praying silently, actually. When he answered, she breathed in deep. "Ham, it's Fi. I need you to walk away if Grier's around you."

"All right." His voice gave her courage. Warmed her. Pulled all her strength to the front, beyond her fear. "You okay?"

She mouthed the words, *he's gone* to Tyler. "Yeah. I'm fine. I need you to do something for me."

"Where are you, Fiona?"

She chuckled. "No worries. I'm just on a little spring break. I'll explain as soon as I see you." *Spring break* was the only clue she'd been able to give. Maybe he'd remember their talk about the Easter she'd spent at Lauderdale. Hopefully. If not, she'd figure a plan B. "I need you to open the right-hand drawer of my desk, pull it all the way out."

She couldn't hear more than his breathing. "All right."

Her heart thumped wildly, hurt even as she thought of Grier and the danger she was putting him in. "On the back of the drawer is a little black book. It has the safe combination in it." There was no real reason for him to open the safe. Everything she needed was in the zip drive she kept with her at all times. Right now, it was in a plastic bag at the bottom of the diaper wipes container. "Go to the safe, open it."

It was a push-button safe, he only had to enter in a few digits and the door latch would release. "I'm gonna find you, Fiona."

"Yeah, I know. Leave the cash alone." She paused and breathed then smiled at Sedotal and rolled her eyes. If ever a woman deserved an award for acting, it was Fiona Strong-Owen. "See the black ledger?"

"Yeah."

"Ham, I need *you* and nobody else to take it to the Boston Monument. Tomorrow. Five o'clock." She took a breath. "No, not the Bunker Hill Massacre statue. God, you love that place. The Boston Monument." Oh, God. He had to get the veiled messages. They were planning to massacre Hamilton if he showed. Grier and every other Screaming Demon needed to be present, armed and ready to die if Hamilton was even to have a chance. "You'll get instruction from there." She hung up and held the phone palm up.

"You *are* cold. Thought that one was your best friend."

She shrugged. "I like my baby more."

Sedotal slung an arm around her shoulders and pulled her in to kiss her temple. "*Our* baby for as long as you're a good girl and play by my rules. Don't forget that."

God, she hoped like hell Grier understood, remembered at least. "So, we're on the move now?"

He chuckled. "You are, sweetheart." He clucked his tongue and her heart sank. "Too many people know about this place, and my girl on the inside hasn't checked in all day. So, I have to assume she's been compromised. Shame too. I liked her." His sigh wasn't so much disappointment as contentment. "But I think you'll be a good replacement." If he was stupid enough to believe her act, even if she'd played it like Meryl Streep, for sure she'd be able to out-smart him.

As much out of curiosity as because her list of names felt a little light, she smiled. "Is it Autumn?" That bitch showed up with Kale, Sedotal's man she'd had to kill, and she'd been Grier's ex, so Fiona wouldn't really have minded if it was her name added to the kill list.

He chuckled. "No. And I don't care what kind of little tricks you use. You're not getting it out of me." Oh fuck. He was acting like some teenager in love, trying to charm her, use his good looks and the smile that made her stomach turn to sweet-talk her. And his fucking finger was a little too close to the brand on her thigh. Yeah. He'd be losing that one first.

But she smiled and leaned in. "You don't know what tricks I have up my short little skirt."

She closed her eyes and went to her happy place when he leaned in to kiss her. He had breath like a toilet and thank God, he ended it soon. "You're just gonna have to wait to show me because I have to get back to Pine Hill."

That meant Fiona had a day or so to figure out the rest of her plan, so she didn't have to go all-in with Sedotal. She smiled and started thinking.

GRIER STARED AT THE PHONE. Oh, just to hear her voice, to know she was safe filled his gut with a warmth he didn't think he'd ever feel again. His gut told him she'd been trying to tell him something. *Just on a little spring break.* And the ledger turned out to be nothing more than a journal from her youth. So, he knew the call was more for his benefit than for whatever reason she was supposed to call.

Hamilton stared at him from across the desk. "What did she say?"

No harm in telling Hamilton. And maybe if he said the words out loud, he could make some sense of them. "That she was on spring break, that you're supposed to take this to the Boston Monument tomorrow at five and that she knows you love the Boston Massacre statue better." She'd also said she was fine. And that was the only thing that let him take a solid breath.

"A code, right?"

"Which means Sedotal is with her right now. But he'll be back here at five tomorrow. So, she'll be alone or guarded by someone else." That much wasn't rocket science. If something was going down in Boston, no way would Sedotal risk not being there to see it. "He wouldn't bring her with him. Too risky, right?"

Hamilton shrugged and sighed. "Yeah, which means we have tomorrow to find her."

"Yeah." His wife and baby were in danger. And he had twenty-four hours or less to find them. He had to figure this out. "Okay. Does spring break mean anything to you?" But even as he spoke, Fiona's voice laid over Mia's in his head. "He took her to that fishing shack."

"Thought you didn't believe Mia."

He didn't want to believe her, wanted to kill her as much as he wanted her to be right. "I have to."

"And if it's a trap?"

Of course, it was a trap, but it was his only chance. His only lead. "I'm taking Sage."

"You held a gun to his head. Then you punched him. I don't think he's your ally." Hamilton had a valid point.

"Yeah. But the girl means something to him. And once we show up, Sedotal will know she told us where to go. He'll have my back as long as I have hers." He nodded at Hamilton, satisfied with the plan, such as it was.

"Do you have hers?"

Grier nodded. "I think I have to. Keep her safe."

"Oh no. You're not going anywhere without me."

As much as Grier would love to have Hamilton along, there was security in having Hamilton ride beside him into whatever danger they faced, he needed him here, taking the ledger to the… massacre. God, his woman was a genius. He stared at Hamilton and smiled, shaking his head. "You have to stay here. Sedotal and his goons are gonna be waiting for you and we're going to give them a nice big surprise." As soon as he saw Fiona, he'd never let her go again. Ever.

As soon as Hamilton was on board with the plan and walked out to share his instruction with the others, Grier went to the cells for Sage and Mia.

He leaned against the wall opposite their cell doors, watched the girl try to clean the wound over Sage's eye with a torn piece of her shirt. Neither bothered to look at him. Even when he spoke. "Fiona called." Still nothing. And to be the guy who held their lives in his hands, he expected more. "I think she's at the fishing shack you mentioned." She glanced at him then quickly away, so he continued. "Since you helped me, I'm not going to let anything happen to you. All right?"

She turned, hands on her hips to glare at him. "Sage didn't betray you."

"I know."

Now Sage looked at him. "Then why am I still in a cell?"

Grier chuckled. "Because I forgot the key." And he had.

Mia nodded and pulled a hairpin out of the bun at the back of her head. She unlocked her door and walked out then unlocked Sage's. Sage stared at her, mouth slightly open. "If you could do that the whole time…"

She smiled at Sage then Grier. "You might not trust me, but I trust you, Grier."

Grier shook his head and walked beside her to the stairs. "Risky, since five minutes ago, I was going to have you killed."

"But you didn't."

Sage limped behind them. "Don't worry about me. You two just go on. I'll just crawl up the steps."

Grier went back to help Sage. "What happened to your leg?" He needed Sage in one piece.

"Ham." Enough said.

"Can you ride?" In the absence of Kye, he needed Sage.

"I could ride with two broken legs."

Oh, thank God. It was going to be one long night.

And he watched every second tick off the clock until they had all the details arranged. Then it was time for a nap, and he wasn't in the mood to argue with Hamilton who had insisted. He wanted to get on the road, find his woman and his daughter and get them back home where he could watch them, never let them go. But Hamilton made sense. A long ride, probably a gunfight or some kind of confrontation was coming, and he would need to be alert. What Hamilton couldn't control was Grier's brain and its inability to shut down and let the sleep come.

At one in the morning, they took off. And by four-thirty, a third bike joined them. Kye had come.

6

Fiona's list grew. Asshat, Tyler Sedotal, Body Odor Boy, and Sewer Breath. And that was just the start. The last two, her newest escorts, hadn't called each other by name, and even if they had, the monikers Fiona had blessed them with fit better than anything anyone else could call them. Sewer Breath had thrown her, none too gently, into the back of an SUV, then blindfolded her with what smelled like BO Boy's sock and they drove for what felt like days. And one of them snored, hopefully not while he was driving, but she couldn't be certain because of the blindfold. Fortunately, the baby had slept right up to the minute the car screeched to a halt. Sewer Breath pulled Fiona out of the car and yanked the blindfold off her head. "Where are we?"

He ignored her question and shoved her toward an

old plantation house in the middle of a lawn that was both badly in need of a mow and stretched as far as she could see in every direction, broken only by the narrow drive the car had taken. It was one of those two-story houses with white siding and black shutters and most of the windows were broken out, but in its day, it had probably been something much more impressive than now.

The porch was missing boards and the steps creaked and groaned as she walked up. BO Boy carried the baby seat and diaper bag, huffing and puffing like London had gained a couple of hundred pounds on their trip while Sewer Breath pushed open a squeaking door.

Fiona waited for him to catch up and she took the carrier and the diaper bag, and he smiled. "Thanks, babe."

If she never heard that word again, *babe,* it would be a couple of years too soon. They'd stopped calling her Fiona or Princess a few hundred miles ago. But so far, they'd kept their hands to themselves, so there was that, at least.

She didn't speak but walked into the house in front of him. Moth eaten curtains billowed in the light breeze and the air chilled Fiona so that she set the baby down, dug through the diaper bag, and pulled out a blanket to wrap around London. She changed her diaper and fed her as she walked to a window and looked out. Nothing to the north or east but lawn. Not a single clue to tell her where they'd driven.

There had to be a way out of there. Even if she couldn't hear what her escorts were talking about, she could tell they were worried. Sewer Breath talked with his hands and he was gesturing like an air traffic controller who'd taken a bit too much speed. BO Boy chewed his thumbnail and if Fiona would've cared enough to look, she would have bet he was bleeding.

She'd had about enough of both of them. She watched them, pretending she wasn't, keeping her head down, nuzzling the baby with her chin. But she didn't miss anything. Not Sewer Breath shaking the phone at BO Boy, not the hiss of his words, not the way he slammed out of the room, flinging the door shut behind him. BO Boy pursed his lips and blew out his breath then turned to face her.

"He's going to get food."

Fiona nodded but didn't speak. She needed to know more about him before she decided whether to play him tough or to play him sweet. Not that she had time to spend figuring it out. She didn't even have a coin to flip to decide. "He's not very nice to you, huh?"

"He's the boss right now. He doesn't have to be nice." But he cleared his throat and narrowed his eyes. Those words hurt.

"Why's he the boss? You don't seem like you need someone telling you what to do."

He scoffed. "I don't." He pushed his chest out and lifted his chin. Oh, yeah. She had him now.

"I'm just saying. I think you deserve some respect. And I'd…" Oh, Lord. She needed strength. "…be happy to tell Ty I think you deserve better than being that asshole's whipping boy."

"I ain't nobody's whipping boy." There was some defiance. Just what she needed.

"Don't tell me. Tell him. He's the one talking down to you, right?" She shifted her head to the other side. "My guys know who I trust. No doubt. And when I'm with Ty, I'll make sure his guys do, too." He rolled his eyes. "You think I don't have pull with him? I didn't spend all those hours in that cabin with him sucking his dick." Thank God. "We were planning. Plotting. Figuring out how to make you boys as rich as my boys." This kid was buying every word. "You want me to tell him you should be one of the guys in the inner circle, I will."

"And what do I have to do for you?"

"Again, it's what I can do for you." She leaned forward and moved the baby to her other breast, telling herself she would do what she had to do to protect London and if that meant a couple of peep shows to a kid who'd probably never even seen a woman's boob before, then it would be worth it.

"What can you do for me?"

God help her.

"GODDAMMIT!" Grier tossed the table, the only piece of furniture in the room, on its side and yanked the baby's stuffed bunny, the one Jez had bought and had London's name stitched into the ear, off the wall where Sedotal had nailed it with a note. *Too late!*

His stomach rolled and fury vibrated through his guts. If that son of a bitch hurt Fiona or his baby, Grier was going to kill him so slowly. Kye had called in a few of his old Florida friends and a couple of guys walked in behind Sage. "She's not here."

The guy beside Sage nodded. "We've been watching the place since Kye called. They moved her last night before we got here. Or she wasn't here."

Grier growled and flung the bunny toward him. "She was here." They'd probably passed her on the fucking road and didn't know it. And now they'd lost her. He stared at Grier. "Call your woman and find out if Sedotal has anywhere else he uses." Sage pulled his phone from his pocket and walked out. At least Grier knew she hadn't led them on a wild goose chase.

One of Kye's friends, a different one, walked out behind Sage and the first one stepped closer to Grier.

"I'll ask around. See if anybody knows these guys or where we can find them."

Grier nodded because the words were caught in his throat. He couldn't imagine the horrors Tyler would inflict on Fiona. And he couldn't let himself think of them. Not now. Not if he wanted to survive.

"They took your old lady and your kid?" He handed the bunny back to Grier. "South Beach has your back." Grier nodded and the guy, Tony Sonoma, gave his shoulder a squeeze. "We'll help you find her."

Sage walked back in and came to stand by Grier. "Mia doesn't know of anywhere else they would take her, but…" Grier's heart ached, felt as if it didn't have the strength to keep beating. "Maybe we should fly back and be there for the meet with Ham."

Grier shook his head. He needed to think. Think like Sedotal, a man he didn't know well enough to figure out. Only one thing he knew for certain. "He won't bring Fiona there. It would be too risky. If she managed to get away or hurt, he loses his leverage. He wouldn't take that chance." At least, not if he was smart, and this son of a bitch always seemed to manage to stay a step ahead.

Grier looked around the cabin. Sedotal had kept her here. In this shithole of a place. And no way she wasn't ready to kill him for keeping her there, and Grier for letting Sedotal get to her and probably Sage and a handful of other people connected with this fiasco.

One of Sonoma's guys walked in. "I got a line on your girl. Guy down the beach said a black Escalade pulled out of here in a hurry middle of the night last night escorted by a few bikes."

Fuck. That meant they had a hell of a head start. They could've been anywhere by now. Grier's world narrowed. His stomach clenched and his chest heaved. They'd never find her. If anything happened to Fiona and London.…

He looked at Sage. "We need one of their guys."

Sage nodded. "And in about an hour we know where a bunch of them will be." He filled Tony in then looked back at Grier. "I'll call Hamilton."

Hamilton would be busy. "Call Jim and tell him to have Carl wait back with his bow. I need one of those fuckers, preferably someone close to Sedotal. Somebody who rides in with him, not with the group." As Sage walked out to make the call, Grier yelled after him. "And everybody makes sure Ham gets out alive." If not, not only would Fiona kill him, but Sedotal would think he had won this battle.

Kye watched from the corner of the room, leaning with his shoulder in the corner. There was no one Grier trusted more than Kye, no one else he could count on, except maybe Fiona. "You know, Grier, I was thinking. Why would they keep a place like this, you think?"

The last thing Grier wanted to do was play a round

of Jeopardy with Kye, but he also knew Kye was a man who didn't waste words. He had a point to make. But Grier had too much going on in his head to make sense of someone else's thoughts. "I don't know. Storage? Kidnapping?"

"Probably both, but a place like this... on the water..." He shrugged. "I would bet he uses this place for deliveries. Drugs. Women. Guns. That's why there isn't furniture." He stared. "And if history has taught us anything, these bastards like their tunnels. I'm not saying there are any, but... might be worth doing a little digging." He chuckled. "See what I did there?"

"You're a comic genius." One with a big beautiful brain. "But you're right."

Kye walked out and Sonoma glanced at Grier. "Makes sense. There's been movement on the streets I couldn't pinpoint. Some of my girls went missing and a few shipments came up short." He pulled out his cell and swiped through a few screens then sent a text. "I'll keep a couple of guys out here, watching. If there's somebody trying to take on South Beach territory, I'll end 'em."

Thank God for Kye. Without him, Grier and Sage would be in this alone. Now, he had about thirty guys searching the property, offering to help him take care of his business. "I need my wife back first. And my kid."

"You bet." Sonoma stared down at his phone. "I have one of my guys checking black Escalades on the traffic cams and another checking tolls. I'll get a direction, you can put money on that. And if we find anything, you're the first call."

Sage poked his head in the door. "Hey, Grier. Come have a look."

Grier and Sonoma walked outside the cabin. The whole place reeked of fish and ocean and Grier just wanted to go home, with Fiona. There were no tunnels, but Kye had found a hatch. Crude. Just a few boards nailed together with a lock and a small metal ring on top.

His mind flashed back to the explosion, booby-trapped merchandise stolen from the Demons by Sedotal and his gang. They'd moved Fiona for a reason, and Grier had to believe they knew Mia had been turned to the Demon side and if they knew it, no way they would've left anything important behind. Not without making sure whoever found it met his maker. Or maybe they'd buried Fiona alive. Knew he would come. Left her there for him to find. Oh, God. He needed to throw up.

Sage had his gun pointed at the lock. Grier pushed his hand down. Enough lives had been lost because of him. And if anyone was going to die for Fiona, it should be him. "Wait. I'm gonna do it." He pulled his Glock and aimed.

7

If this fucking guy touched her tit one more time, Fiona was going to tear his goddamned hand off and shove it up his ass. They'd been in this damned cold house since sun-up and she'd been fondled, badly, about a thousand times since. But she smiled as he stroked the valley between her breasts. Again. "So, what were you two arguing about this time?" So far, her dumb and dumber captors had argued over everything from food to who was going to watch Fiona and the baby while the other went for provisions. They'd come to blows over that one and BO Boy had won. Just as she'd hoped.

She dropped her hand into his lap and walked her fingers up his thigh toward his zipper. He caught her hand and laid it over his dick, then squeezed. She resisted the urge to dig her nails in, but not by much. "I forgot to load something into the truck when we left Daytona."

He cupped her boob like a stress ball. She bit back a growl and smiled. "Well, maybe what's his name should've loaded it. You were busy taking care of me." She let her hand close over him again and let her voice drop to a purr. "Too bad Ty left that hands-off rule. Feels like you could show a girl a good time." She swallowed back a mouthful of bile.

His hand slipped under the hem of her shirt, and he tugged at her waistband. He was going for the finish line. "He doesn't have to know."

Before he got far enough for her to have to yank out his windpipe, the door swung open and he jerked away, hopped to his feet, and adjusted his dick.

"What the fuck are you doing?" Sewer Breath charged into the room and grabbed BO by the throat. He shoved him against the wall and held him. "Tyler said no one touches her." Fiona didn't see him pull the gun, but she heard the mechanical click of the hammer and no way could she have missed the glint of silver in the moonlight as he pressed it against BO's head.

Oh no. He couldn't kill the kid. Not after all the work she'd put in. "Boys. Boys. Boys." She stood, fighting the ties around her ankles. "Hey. He didn't do anything. We were talking is all. He was… telling me about what it would be like to be an Omen. That's all."

Though BO couldn't speak, he nodded.

Fiona hopped a couple of steps closer. She wanted that fucking gun so bad, she considered choking Sewer Breath with the short line of rope he'd left to give her enough slack to be able to feed and hold the baby. But until she was sure of BO's loyalty to her, she couldn't risk making a move. But BO's eyes were bulging, and he couldn't breathe. She had to do something. She focused all of her energy, all of her power on throwing her hands over his head, yanking him against her body, and securing the rope against his windpipe.

BO stumbled and the gun went off, caught him in the cheek and he went down. But so did the gun. And Fiona was weak, hadn't worked out in months. Her arms burned with her effort and Sewer Breath had his hand on the back of her head, yanking handfuls of her hair like his life depended on it. Finally, he pulled her over his shoulder, and she landed on her back on the floor in a pool of BO's blood. Any breath she'd had left escaped in a whoosh and she struggled for another. Sewer Breath was free, rubbing his neck and holding the gun on her.

"Stupid move, bitch." He backhanded her and her head twisted to the side. "Now look." He jabbed the revolver, a pearl-handled six-shooter, at the prone and lifeless body of her other captor.

Fiona spit out a mouthful of blood and a tooth before he came closer, arm pulled back for another strike, and the world went dark.

* * *

FIONA DIDN'T KNOW how long she was out, but she knew she was freezing and the baby was crying. Her hands were tied behind her back and BO was still sprawled on the floor with a large red circle of blood under his head. The entire left side of her face throbbed and she was pretty sure he'd broken something in there since she couldn't move without pain. She needed to sit up and feed the baby, but she couldn't do anything with her hands tied behind her. And Sewer Breath was nowhere she could see from her one partially opened eye. She tried to turn her head, to get a better view, but she couldn't lift her cheek from the floor. Oh, God.

Pain ricocheted through her as she tried to slide her legs up so she could get onto her knees and try to get to the baby. But everything hurt. Nothing worked or moved the way she wanted. And the baby continued to cry, to wail. Fiona tried to move her mouth, to speak enough to try to comfort the baby, but her jaw wouldn't move either.

Every move cost her a gasp of pain and every gasp of pain cost her a moment of clarity. No way she was going to make it through this. And the baby... oh, God, London. Tears leaked out of her eyes and she let them fall. She gritted her teeth—at least she thought she did, she couldn't tell—and pushed her forehead against the floor. With every ounce of strength she had, she pulled her knees across the floor, leaving skin behind, and didn't stop until they touched her stomach then her chest. Now all she had to do was raise up. It took three tries before she made herself sit upright. Her head swam and once she was finally straightened, her body revolted and she heaved, almost fell over again, but somehow, maybe through sheer will, her body supported her.

Oh, God. She just needed to get to the baby, hold her, feed her, let her know Mommy hadn't given up. The footsteps came with some speed toward her and she fell back onto her ass, cowering, curling in on herself to protect what was left of her face and body. A pair of arms slipped under her knees and behind her back and she leaned her head against his chest, hoping, praying it was Grier, but the small part of her left knew it wasn't. Not his smell. Not his arms. Not his chest.

More tears leaked out of her eyes as he laid her on a bed or a car seat, something not as hard as a floor anyway. In the distance, a foggy sound-clouded distance, she could hear London still wailing. And then the first shot rang out and Fiona's eyes snapped open. She struggled for focus, to figure out what was going on. It took a minute to realize her arms were free and she was holding London. She shifted, trying to move her feet. They were still tied, but she had her baby and that was enough.

THE INFORMATION WAS SHODDY. And came at a cost. Sonoma and a group of his men had traveled with Grier, Sage and Kye to Atlanta, found the run-down plantation house and the twenty or so men Sedotal had left behind. If only they'd gotten the information sooner, but Hamilton hadn't been able to break the guy Carl had shot with his bow. But Sonoma's guys came through. By the time the gunfight in Boston was over, Sonoma's guy had a property address, a satellite image and enough firepower to blow up half the east coast. And still, the Omens managed to get away with Fiona. How a giant black Escalade had managed to get past them, Grier couldn't guess, but all they'd left behind were some trigger-happy shooters with more ammo than aim. Sonoma and his guys ended the fight quickly and dead men littered the ground. Sonoma's men left a lot of blood in their wake.

Kye kicked one of the Omen bodies and the body

groaned up at him. A bright red bloodstain continued to spread across his stomach, and Kye knelt to hold his hand over the wound. "Where'd they take her?"

"Who cares? She's not gonna live to see the sunrise."

Grier's chest clenched, and he wanted to pummel the guy. Instead, he knelt beside Kye and jerked the guy's head toward him. "Tell me where she is!" He pushed Kye away and stuck his thumb into the hole in the bastard's gut.

"Probably on her way back to Pine Hill." For being on his way out of this world, the fucking guy had a lot of balls. And there really wasn't any reason why he shouldn't have been so gutsy. Not like Grier posed much of a threat. He couldn't even protect his own wife and his kid. This guy had nothing to be afraid of. Except Grier. Who didn't have anything left to lose.

Still, what the son of a bitch said didn't make sense. Why would Sedotal drag her up and down the east coast if he was just going to bring her home? It had to mean something. "What does he want?"

"Fuck you, man." The guy's breath hitched and a gurgle in his throat said he didn't have much time left. But goddamned if he was going into the light before Grier found out what he needed to know.

Grier twisted his thumb and fought a wave of nausea as the guy screamed and writhed against the pain. "Tell me." He needed to know, and he'd do whatever it took. "What does he want?"

The guy's eyes rolled back, and he gasped softly. "Your club. Your woman. Your life." Another gurgle and he grabbed Grier's arm. "Help me. Please."

Grier looked up at Kye and nodded then waited until Kye put a bullet in the guy's head before he turned and yelled at the horizon. "Fuck!" He let out a string of curses and for the first time considered giving it all up. Not fighting Sedotal but letting him have whatever he wanted as long as he returned Fiona and the baby unharmed. No heroics, just a man getting his wife and child back.

He almost laughed at the absurdity of it. Two years ago, he'd been happily sunning on a beach in Belize, living his life, never thinking of a wife or a child. Then Fiona had shown up, her fiery hair blazing in the sun, her eyes flashing with so much hatred and anger he'd thought she planned to shoot right outside Kye and Eli's house. Somehow, they'd ended up married and it still boggled his mind. Luckiest thing that ever happened to him, even though Max and Fiona had forced his hand. And now they had London, as beautiful as her mother.

Kye glanced at him then away while the other men checked bodies, collected weapons and money from the men on the ground. "We're going to find her."

"What if it's too late?" He hadn't said the words out loud, hadn't dared to let himself fall apart, but only his skin was holding him together and he could feel it splintering. He wanted to sink into himself and let go.

Kye squeezed his shoulder. "It won't be. You have to believe that."

Grier wanted to believe everything would be okay, but the sun came up every morning and went down every night and still, Fiona was out there going through God knew what. Every muscle and cell he had screamed in agony brought on by his mind, by the pain in his gut and the ache in his heart. Thinking of her out there, with… them, with Tyler Sedotal. His breath came in short bursts and he doubled over. Oh, God. He couldn't do this. Not without her. Not without them.

Kye held him up. "Stop it. Don't do this here. You keep your shit together until there aren't twenty guys around watching you fall apart." He shook Grier by the shoulders, but the words didn't matter anymore. Nothing mattered; he'd failed her. Even if they found her now, she'd been through too much, would blame him, maybe as much as he blamed himself. Probably not. Either way, he deserved whatever she said or did to him. And they'd never be able to go back to the way they were as long as they both knew he'd failed her.

Kye gave him another shake. "Take a breath and rein it in. We're going to get them back, and that's all you need to think about right now, you hear me?" Grier didn't answer and Kye shook him again. "We're going to find her. Say it, Grier. Say it!"

"We're going to find her." But he didn't believe it anymore.

iona could smell Pine Hill. The air here was charged with something the coast didn't have. He'd brought her back home. Dangerous and stupid for him. And she'd had enough. The baby cooed in her chair as the Escalade slowed and stopped. They'd forced her into the back, hadn't let her up in the four or so hours since they'd stopped for a bathroom break. Her legs were cramped and her stomach sick, but her anger pushed her on. Anger and the desire to get back to Grier.

The back hatch opened, and Sedotal came around to help her out. She stood and it took her a minute to find her strength, for her muscles to cooperate and her knees to hold her up. He had her hands tied in front of her and she eyed the gun in his waistband. Soon. She would get it and blow him into the thousand little pieces of shit he was. And then she'd find a really good plastic surgeon and get this shit cut off her body. But first, she had work to do.

He bent to loosen the ties at her feet so she could walk. When she was free, he straightened and put his hands on her shoulders. "Sorry about all this, babe. As soon as you hold your end of the bargain and Grier's dead, we won't need all this anymore."

She smiled. Her face still ached, and she was pretty sure her jaw was broken, and she still had a concussion, but no way would she surrender to the pain. She held onto her anger like a life raft. More than anything she wanted to know what happened to old Sewer Breath after he'd inflicted this pain. She turned her head as another black SUV pulled in. Two guys climbed out and yanked a third from the back seat. He couldn't stand on his own, couldn't even hold his head up.

Good. Not like she could've inflicted the pain she wanted to, the pain he deserved. Sedotal smiled. "I brought him back here for you." He chuckled and wrapped both arms around her. "I thought you might like to do the honors yourself." He kissed her forehead and winked when he pulled back. He picked up the baby seat. "Come to papa."

This fucking psycho had some crazy fantasy about playing house with her and London. And she'd let him have it right up until the minute she put a bullet in his head. Having him hold London though made her stomach twist into a knot, but she swallowed back the animosity and pictured Grier. The only thing that kept her going through that entire drive back to Pine Hill from the plantation was imagining Grier riding in and swooping her and London back to safety. Not exactly a fairytale, but as close as a girl like Fiona would ever get.

Sedotal carried the baby seat in one hand and guided her into the back of a small block building. He hadn't spoken to her at all since he'd returned, and she was dying to know what happened when Hamilton went to the monument. If he was okay. If any of her guys had been hurt. She sucked in a few breaths through her nose and willed the pain away as she opened her lips to speak. "Did you get the ledger?"

He shook his head and smiled. "No. But I think you knew I wouldn't. I think you knew your boys and those Maniacs—" another club Hamilton or Grier must've called in, "—would be waiting." He laughed. "It's okay. I expected nothing less. I actually expected more. But it kept your boys busy enough for me to get into your clubhouse and get what I needed."

It was all a set-up. She should've seen that coming. And now she felt stupid on top of the pain in her face. She could only nod expecting another backhand or something equally painful, but he walked beside her as peacefully as if he was leading his family home. When he drew his hand away to shove it into his pocket and pulled out her zip drive, her heart sank.

"I took your computer before I knew you had this. Pretty genius hiding place. If I hadn't decided to let you sleep and change the baby myself, I would've never known. But even I knew diaper wipe boxes don't rattle. Too bad, though. If you would've told me, I wouldn't have had to shred your office." He shrugged. "I always liked your chair though." He popped the door open and guided her inside what looked like an old dance studio.

In front of her, a wall of mirrors projected her reflection and she almost vomited at the sight of herself. Or rather, at the sight of someone she assumed was her but was horribly misshapen and every shade of purple on the color wheel.

The floor was a high-polished light wood and a ballet bar was screwed into the wall opposite the mirrors. In the middle, he'd put her white leather desk chair and the furry rug she'd had in her office at the Demon clubhouse.

She stared at herself, even turning her head to see the still angry red welt on her neck, the brand he'd put there. As he moved further into the room, she closed her eyes, imagining shooting him in the heart and making him watch himself die in front of the mirrors. The thought gave her enough determination to walk further into the room.

"Sit." He nodded to the chair then squatted to unlatch the baby from her chair and carry her to Fiona. "I took care of her for you. I had to give her formula, but she took it fine."

He'd fed her baby? Formula? What the hell? She cocked her eyebrow, and he smoothed a hand over London's head. "You couldn't feed her, babe. I didn't know what else to do."

Fiona swallowed back a batch of angry tears and nodded. "Thank you."

Every word hurt her face, but the pain kept her focused on her objective, made her remember the names on her list. Asshat. BO Boy, but he was already dead. Sewer Breath. Tyler Sedotal. "I'm going to get some ice for your face. Then, we need to talk."

She nodded and he disappeared down a hallway. She could've tried to run, but there was no way she would make it out past him and however many guys he had outside guarding the building. She didn't know for sure anyone was out there, but it was what she would've done, so she had to wait, bide her time, make a good plan.

Oh, who was she kidding? At this rate, she'd have to wait for a rescue, for Grier. Her eyes misted and this time, she couldn't hold the tears back. One dripped off her chin and landed on the baby's nose. Fiona wiped it away and cuddled London closer to her. "Daddy'll be here soon. We just have to hang on."

And for all her faith in Grier, she picked the wrong time to say it. Sedotal walked in, his eyes dark, dangerous, and angry. "Daddy, huh?" He threw the ice bag at her and she hunched to protect London. The ice hit her in the ear and the jaw. She cried out and he advanced. "I'm going to take everything you have, and I'm going to make you watch me kill him."

Fiona closed her eyes, the pain bigger than she could manage, but she held onto London, wouldn't let go again.

* * *

BASEBALL PLAYERS HAD THEIR TRADITIONS. Letting the beard grow. Not washing the jersey. Keeping the cleats from winning year to winning year. But when things went bad, there were haircuts and hot shaves, new jerseys, new equipment, something that made them believe this would be the change that worked. Grier needed one of those. Something to break his string of bad luck.

He'd managed to catch a few hours' sleep and now he needed to work on the things that kept the club going, the shipments and the payments and the assignments. But all he wanted to do was find Fiona and London, bring them home and spend every day making this up to his wife and daughter.

He'd put Carl and Jim on the street to rattle cages, shakedown whoever they could find. Hamilton stood beside him at the bar, Autumn wiping the counter on her side. Hamilton nodded to her as she served Sage a beer. "Not the same without Jez back there."

Grier nodded. "I know. Couldn't save her either, could I?" His blood burned with anger and he clenched his fist on the bar.

"I'm not saying that."

"True though, right?" He narrowed his eyes into a glare. "Everybody's thinking it. You're thinking it."

Sage gripped his shoulder. "Nobody believes Jez dying is your fault."

He shook off Sage's hand and turned. Probably not smart to pick a fight in a room full of guys who'd hated him for a while, only liked him because he'd married up, and probably now hated him again. But he needed this, to clear his head the only way he knew how. He needed to throw a punch, take a punch, get the bad out to make room for the good. And no time like the present. He pushed back his stool and shoved Sage.

Sage put up his hands and backed away. Then Hamilton stood and walked out. "Goddammit. Get back here."

This time, the hand on his shoulder whirled him

around, and he swung his fist in a wide arc that caught Kye on the chin. A man who understood. Kye swung back his fist landed against Grier's jaw, and Grier jerked backward. They exchanged swing for swing, pushing each other further into the room then back toward the door until they exploded through and ended up on the concrete outside.

Kye leveled his shoulder into Grier's midsection and shoved him into the wall. "You need more?" He moved back, his breaths in short puffs that matched Grier's.

"I messed this all up." Grier wiped a stream of blood from his lip with the back of his hand.

"And now, you'll fix it." He opened his mouth and stretched his skin. "Had to aim for my face." He walked back toward the clubhouse. "Come on. Let's get cleaned up and figure out what to do next."

Grier had thought a fight would get the anger out, help him to clear his head enough he could form a plan, and he would know what to do. Sadly, it solved nothing. "Go ahead. I'll be there in a little while." He wanted to get out of there, find a place that didn't remind him of her and her perfume and all the things about her Tyler Sedotal was probably busy trying to destroy.

He climbed on his bike before Kye could stop him then zoomed out of the lot. He needed time. The business would wait long enough for him to return. He drove through Southie to the old neighborhood, where he'd grown up in a group home after running away from the last foster home. Not that the group home was better. But he'd found a way out of there, been smart enough to figure out how to stay in school and still not have to go back there.

The old group home had been converted to a dance studio that was no longer open. The windows, high on the walls, were boarded up and the whole place was enclosed by a makeshift fence. He sat out front staring, remembering the time the O'Hally brothers had locked him in the basement with the old, creaking boiler and no light. He'd been ten and stuck down there for two days before anyone found him. He also remembered the day Kye showed up. Thank God for Kye. Together, they were unstoppable, but then he'd been fostered out. He still came back for Grier, though, helped him get out of there.

For a dollar, maybe less, Grier would've set the old place on fire, but it was mostly concrete and block so it would just become another eyesore in a neighborhood with way too many eyesores. He stared at the building and through a crack in one of the boards on the front window, he saw light. Like electricity light.

He crossed the street on foot and made short work of climbing the fence. A long time ago, he'd gone inside, when it was a dance studio. Walls had been knocked down, the old dirty gray paint had been covered in stark white with red accents, and the dingy carpeted floors had been stripped and covered with a high sheen hardwood. They'd taken out the day room and made it into a shop with racks of sequined costumes and those little skirts ballet dancers wore. Rooms, where he'd endured all manner of torture, had been transformed into a place where kids learned to twirl and tumble. But Grier hadn't been able, even with all the transformation, to see anything but his own memories.

He stayed in the shadows of the building and crossed to the back of the building. The grass was damp on the side and he slipped into a tiny trench full of water and got a boot full of sludge and mud. He couldn't imagine why he'd decided to do this, morbid curiosity maybe, but he moved through the side yard and stopped at the corner of the building and counted. Twelve bikes, three guys outside smoking, one black SUV, and one way out. The math didn't favor Grier, but damned if he was leaving. Not until he knew who was inside this place. He shot a text with the address—one he still remembered—to Kye and Sage. Then he snapped a couple of pictures—bikes, guys, the license plate, before he crept back around the building to his bike.

There were no clubs in this part of Southie. This was gang territory because those guys didn't mind the "up and coming" aspect of the neighborhood. Motorcycle clubs like the Demons didn't favor so much traffic near their business center. Too risky to run big trucks full of stolen merchandise and black-market drugs down such widely traveled streets. And it wasn't like this was some sort of secluded hideout. This was so close to downtown Southie he could smell the garlic from Alfredo's Italian Kitchen.

If Grier would've had any Spidey senses, they would've been tingling. He didn't want to leave, but he needed intel and he needed to set up on the other side of the building. Not like he could do anything for Fiona, but at least when she returned, he'd be able to tell her he'd done what he could to save her business. No other club was coming to town. Not now.

iona's face would never heal if she couldn't figure out a way to get him to stop hitting her. Every time she looked in the mirror, she had a new bruise or something else that needed stitching up. Now that he'd stopped trying to sleep with her, he'd taken to using her as a punching bag, and it was starting to piss her off.

She looked again in the mirror at her face. Only her eyes appeared to be hers. Nothing else matched the woman she'd been a week ago. And, God as her witness, she would make him pay. She imagined the look on his face when she took the first shot. The thought gave her comfort and she blew out a slow breath. Anything bigger or faster than the shallow inhales and exhales might have killed her. But at least he hadn't taken London or hurt her.

London slept quietly in her seat with Fiona on the floor next to her. He'd taken the chair and the rug and now she had the hard floor and the mirrors and nothing else. Someone brought her food a couple of times a day —energy shakes with lots of protein and a straw since she couldn't open her mouth wide enough to eat—and she had plenty of supplies for the baby. So, there was that.

The door swung open and Tyler stood, same sick smile as usual on his face, same angry eyes glaring at her. "Stand up."

Easier said than done but she used the bar and pulled herself to her feet.

"You think you're pretty smart, don't you?" Normally, Fiona would have answered with a reply that would have let him know she was certainly smarter than him, but she couldn't speak at all anymore. And sarcasm would only make it worse. "Password protection. And my guys can't crack it."

Of course they couldn't. They were little better than circus clowns who'd lost their circus.

She nodded and he jerked his head toward the door. "We're going into the office and if you try anything—" he picked up the baby chair, "—I'm gonna take it out on her. Do you understand?"

She nodded again and walked beside him down the hallway, taking note of the exit door ahead of her and the three other closed doors in the hallway. A camera hung next to the exit.

Tyler unlocked a door with his free hand and pushed Fiona inside ahead of him. The office, little more than a closet, had a wall of screens that each showed a different view of the building, inside and out. Fifteen TVs and some of them showed a split view of the same area from different angles.

Fiona watched the screens for a minute before Tyler grabbed her by the hair and pulled her toward the desk. But she'd seen enough. The outside didn't appear to be guarded although the number of bikes out back indicated that there were men in the building she hadn't seen. She thought of the three hallway doors. Probably, they were behind those.

He pushed her into her desk chair and spun it with his free hand so she was facing her own computer. "Open the file." There were hundreds of files on her computer. Some real, some she'd faked in case of a police raid. She had one smidgeon of a second to decide which to open. He slapped the back of her head. "Open. The file." Fake it was. And once she opened it, she would have a limited amount of time before he discovered her deception.

Even typing hurt, the sound of the keys clicking, the fingers he'd stomped yesterday. But she opened the file and waited while he stared over her shoulder. "Good girl." He pushed her chair back and leaned over her, bracing a hand on each of the chair arms. "You can end all of this right now, you know. All you have to do—" he pushed his knee between hers and shoved hers apart, "—is help me kill Grier. Then we'll merge the clubs and get rid of the trash and we'll run the whole thing together." She would've rolled her eyes, but the pain... or Tyler, would have killed her.

So far, he'd only abused her with fists and boots, but the leer on his face as he pulled down the collar of her shirt for a peek meant she didn't have much time left before he started violating her with his dick. Her stomach rolled, and if she could've opened her mouth, she would've thrown up on his shoes.

He patted her cheek and pain ricocheted around her face into her brain. "Whether you help me or not, I'm going to kill him. I'm giving you the chance to decide which side of the gun you and your baby want to be on."

Her open eye welled with tears. She'd expected to be saved by now. It had been days. Felt like years. And she wasn't far from giving up. If not for the baby...

He took her hand and helped her from the chair. "You can sit over there." He pointed to a chair on the other side of the room. When Fiona tried to pick up the baby carrier and winced, he chuckled. "I forgot to tell you. I got you some help." He walked to the door and poked his head out. Fiona stared at the screens. She wouldn't have seen him if Tyler hadn't walked out of the room, wouldn't have had any hope, but there he was, there they were. Grier and Hamilton and even that damned Kye, looking for all the world like heroes come to save her. The camera barely picked them up, but she would've recognized Grier anywhere.

When the door opened again, she spun away from the screens, the suddenness costing her much-needed breath, but she didn't want Tyler to see her watching the cameras. Her stomach churned as he walked in with some twenty-something woman whose blonde hair was chopped short to match her shorts. She had the same brand on her neck as Fiona and a wild, scared look in her eyes. Young. Stupid. Ready to follow Tyler to the end of the world and let him throw her into the abyss. That was the look she had. Not someone Fiona would be able to count on to help her.

The girl bypassed Fiona and went straight for the baby. She took London out of the car seat and walked around the desk cooing and babbling in a syrupy sweet baby-talk voice.

"I thought you might not be getting enough beauty sleep at night." Tyler brushed his finger over her bruised cheek to her swollen jaw. "You're looking a little rough, so Jade is going to keep the baby overnight."

Fiona shook her head. "No."

He cocked an eyebrow and approached her with his

hand drawn back. Fiona couldn't take another hit to her face and cowered behind her arms. "Please, no." The words reverberated through her head along with the thought of being away from London, the only comfort either of them had in this whole mess.

He dropped his hand as the door to the office slammed open. "Give her the baby." The woman didn't move, and Fiona lifted her head to see the man in the doorway, the man whose gravelly voice reminded her of her own father but whose eyes were all Grier.

Willy Carr walked further into the office and took the baby from Jade, cuddling her close to his chest as he walked toward Fiona. "Aren't you a mess?" Mess was such a nice way to put it. "Did you put up a fight?" Fiona couldn't be sure whether he was talking to her or the baby since he spoke so softly, but she shook her head. "Well, let's get you cleaned up. Some food. Some fresh clothes. A bath. Then we'll talk. Just you and me and this little love." He handed her the baby and looked at Jade. "Take her to your room and help her." The *don't cross me* was implied.

And while Fiona was grateful for his timing, his kindness, and that he'd given her baby back, she knew enough not to trust anyone. Least of all Willy Carr.

* * *

GRIER HADN'T SEEN much movement in the few hours since Carr showed up. No bikes in. No one out. Even the guards disappeared from their posts. He looked at Hamilton. "I'm going in."

"Grier, that's suicide." Kye hissed the words as they stood at the corner of the building.

"I'm tired of sitting here with my dick in my hand while she's in there." He hadn't seen her, but he knew she was there, could feel it in the part of him where he kept his love for her.

Kye spun him around and pushed him against the building, his forearm against Grier's throat. "You don't know she's in there."

"I feel it here." He punched his fist against Kye's chest. "If it was Eli, you'd have shot this place up already."

"And we will, but first, we need help. We need more firepower, more men. You can't go in there alone. You won't make it out. There are at least twenty guys in there and each one of them probably has two guns, a knife and grenade launcher."

Now he was exaggerating. "Then get them here because I'm not waiting much longer."

Hamilton nodded.

And Grier saw the logic. Going in alone, there were a hundred ways it could go wrong, and almost no chance he would walk out alive with his wife and his baby. But if there was one tiny little possibility he could save her a minute's pain, he had to take it. But he held up his hands. He stayed at the side of the building shadowed by the sun. He couldn't see more than the parking lot which was half-full of bikes but without guards.

He didn't know more than he had to get to Fiona and London. Every minute they waited, his imagination rewarded him with some vision of Fiona, some horrid idea of what she was suffering. The panic was real. And Fiona was inside, probably cool and put together, because she didn't lose her shit. Knowing her, she was in there taking names, making lists, and collecting weapons to bust herself out of there. God, he hoped so.

Hamilton tapped Grier's shoulder and motioned toward the house next door. He nodded to Kye who shook his head. He would stay behind which was fine since he wouldn't be welcome in a Demon planning session. They circled around the back of the house and through the side yard to the street, and Grier walked beside Hamilton down the block, just two guys in leather jackets on someone else's turf taking a leisurely stroll. Two guys in leather jackets climbing into the back of a transport truck while two more guys in leather jackets stood look-out because that didn't look conspicuous at all.

Grier took a seat between Hamilton and Dave. No one looked at him and that was probably for the best. He wasn't strong enough to hide what he felt right now. And one way or another it ended today.

The crates they were sitting on were full of guns - rifles, shotguns, automatics of every make and model. They brought him comfort. He stood up. The man in charge. And it was time to take control, time to right the wrongs.

"This isn't about the club or the business." His voice came with confidence. "It's about me. They want me." The plan sat somewhere just out of his grasp, but he had their attention and he needed to keep it. "And I want Fiona and London safe." A couple of random nods. "I need to go in."

"You plan to just walk in the front door?" Hamilton stared at him. "They'll kill all three of you."

That wasn't the endgame plan. Sedotal didn't want Grier dead. Not until he made him suffer. He wanted to take everything. Fiona and the baby. Jez. The club. Then he would kill Grier and not one minute before. And he didn't have the club yet.

"No. He needs the connections that Fiona has. The names, the computer, won't do any good without her." This was thinking out loud, spit-balling. "And she won't give them anything if they hurt the baby." Yes. He knew that. But the damned plan. He just couldn't get a hold on it. "She won't let them hurt the baby." God, he needed sleep, to clear his head, figure out what to do. "I have to go in."

Hamilton shook his head. "No."

"She needs me." She would be waiting for him. For him, not for Hamilton or Sage or Dave. She would be waiting for her husband to save her. He would walk in, take back what belonged to him and those he belonged to.

"She needs us." Hamilton put a hand on his shoulder. "But we have to go in smart. He's not going to leave her unguarded, not even for a second. You can't give yourself up if it doesn't get her out. There's a better way."

Grier closed his eyes, tried to focus. "No. It has to be me. I'm what they want."

"You've been out here for three days watching that damned building. You haven't eaten, you haven't slept, you're on the edge and you're about to fall over." He banged the front wall of the truck, the wall behind the cab. The truck started and Grier lunged for the door, but Hamilton caught him, pinning his arms to his sides and lifting him off the ground. He couldn't get any purchase, couldn't move. So, he stopped.

"I'll fucking kill you, Hamilton." He growled the words and they had absolutely no effect.

"Maybe, but not today." Hamilton shoved him down onto the crate and stood over him. "Today, you're going home, and you're going to sleep and eat and for God's sake take a shower. Then when your head is clear, you're going to figure out what to do. Jim and that fucking Kye are watching the studio. There's nothing you can do right now."

He'd left Sage with Kye. "Where's Sage?"

Hamilton shook his head. "You sent him to try to get into their security system."

When? When had he done that? He closed his eyes and tried to remember. Why would he think Sage could break into a security system? He listed the things he knew about Sage. Ex-military. Army ranger? Was that right? But before that… he'd been a computer hacker, sentenced by a judge to either enlist or go to jail for a hack into an Air Force drone. Yes. That was why Grier had thought Sage would be able to get into the system.

Right. It was coming back to him. Sage was tech. Intel. Dave was surveillance, death without gunshots. Hamilton, an enforcer. Death with many gunshots. He closed his eyes. He needed… Fiona.

iona stared at the man holding her baby. He'd waited while she cleaned herself up, brought a doctor to see her, medicate her, fix some of what Tyler had damaged. He'd given her the clothes she'd packed for her trip to Belize, and he'd rescued her from another beating.

He stared at her through Grier's eyes, with Grier's smile, even held London in that one-armed way Grier did, firm and secure but with a casualness Fiona had never been able to replicate. "I want you to call my son."

Over the years, Fiona had learned a lot from her father. She'd watched him talk and talk until he gained the confidence of those around him. He used that same method when he was interrogating or torturing whoever was on his receiving end. They got the stories of his youth and somehow, he always managed to find some link between his story and the situation. Maybe it was a skill or a gift or maybe he was just a liar, but he knew what he was doing. Fiona, on the other hand, had no choice but to use silence and hope it worked.

"You look so much like your mother. Or you did until… I'm sorry about Tyler." He walked a full circle around her. "He doesn't understand the nuances yet of this… legacy of ours."

Oh, dear God. He could save this line of shit. Nothing going on here had one damned thing to do with legacies or nuances. This was greed and evil. But she waited.

"My sons. Two sons. One I would have given my life for, the other who would gladly take it." He held out his hand for hers then tucked her fingers in the crook of his arm. "Do you know which one's which?"

She shrugged one shoulder as he handed her the baby and motioned for her to sit on the sofa in the room he'd brought her to. It was smaller than the studio room but furnished like an apartment, complete with a refrigerator and microwave. The furniture was 1970s tacky and about as comfortable as if it had been stuffed with concrete, but she sat and crossed her ankles, glad not to have to worry about being hit. How low she'd sunk.

Carr paced in front of her then came to sit beside her, his knees turned toward hers. "I loved Jezebel more than I loved my own life." He smiled at her. "Loved your dad, too. Good man, that one." Max Strong was a lot of things. A good man wasn't one of them. He'd lied, every day of his life. Cheated. Ran drugs, guns, and women. Broke more laws than he kept. Killed men for smiling wrong or talking to him without the respect he felt he deserved. And goddammit, she missed him. But the last thing she needed was to sit in a room with this nostalgic clown while he waxed poetic about Max and Jez and a club he walked away from.

"What do you want?" She spoke slowly because the pain was there, always there and she couldn't fight that and him.

"Just like your father. To the point." He pushed his legs out straight and leaned back, laced his fingers behind his head. "You are exactly what I expected. Spitting image of your mom, Max's attitude, his toughness." He shifted and looked at her. "I can't let you go. My boys have to work this out because there can only be one club here that takes it all."

Jesus, now he was turning this into some pathetic folk song. Next to batshit crazy in the urban dictionary, they'd have an eight by ten glossy of this fucker. "And what am I, the prize?"

"You're the tool. Your business is the prize. My son thinks he can use your computer to take over your business and your club, but you and I know that without you, without Max's name behind you, there is no business. The contacts he built over the years, the men who trusted him, they won't just fall in line unless you tell them to, unless you're part of the package." He nodded. "Did you know that in the old days when your dad and I disagreed, we fought it out the old-fashioned way?" He rubbed his hand over his jaw then sat up. "That bastard always won. So strong. Funny that he's dead now and I'm not." At least he had the good grace to look ashamed. "Well, not funny ha-ha obviously, but funny in an ironic sense."

"Mm." Not funny in any sense, but she had her baby in her arms and she'd be seeing Grier very soon, so arguing could wait, but she added Carr to her list and focused on Grier. Grier, who wouldn't be dumb enough to come into this place without enough artillery and ammunition to blow it sky-high. Grier, who would save her from this and kill everyone in his path.

Carr stood and walked to the refrigerator. "This isn't how I imagined my life back then."

Had her eyes not been swollen almost shut she would've rolled them. "Picket fences were never in your future." Neither was grandfatherhood.

"And you think they're in yours?" Fiona flinched and hated herself and him for it as his voice climbed a few decibels. "You think you'd be happy being the soccer mom? Fixing the gluten-free lunches and driving carpools and heading the PTA?" He laughed. "Not

Maxwell Strong's daughter." He turned a circle with his arms spread. "This was always your future. Your destiny was to run his club."

It wasn't destiny. It was a knife fight or a gun battle that killed Dhal. A cancer that killed her father. A thousand little accidents and on-purposes that took out one member after another of her father's inner circle and left the club for the next generation. But Carr could have his last moments of delusions. And he could take them straight to hell with him. The thought gave her enough comfort that she almost smiled.

"Would've been Grier's too, had your father and Jez not gone behind my back and hidden him away from me." He shook his head. "She betrayed me with your father."

Fiona tensed. This wasn't a road she could let him walk down. "That was a long time ago."

"Yeah. Water under the bridge." He nodded and looked out the back window. "Could've been a different world if we hadn't all fallen apart. Your dad and I were unstoppable."

Tales of their glory days had been Fiona's bedtime stories—minus the details about Carr with Jez and Grier. Max had hidden things, flat out lied about other things. And still, Max wasn't the worst person in the room. Oh, what she would've done to have Max with her now. He would've known what to do.

"He was the brains. Could negotiate with the best of them." He chuckled. "One time…" She let him go on and pretended to listen but instead surveyed this room. A window. Cabinets that held any number of things she could use as a weapon. She couldn't very well Bruce Lee herself out of here, but she might be able to fend off an attack or two until Grier arrived. On the other hand, the drawers could very well be empty which meant she was in the same position as she'd been earlier. No worse off but with furniture to sit on.

If only her head would stop aching, she might be able to come up with a plan better than rooting through drawers and trying to climb out of a window with her baby in her arms.

"Do you understand how important this is, what's about to happen?" He crouched in front of her. "One of my sons is going to run these clubs and you're going to help one way or the other." Fiona didn't miss the threat, and she nodded although she'd kill Tyler Sedotal herself before she let him run one damned thing. Not that she didn't think Grier could take him. He could. He would. And now all she had to do was wait for him to come.

* * *

GRIER CROUCHED beside the side of the building. Sage beside him. "You fixed the cameras?"

Sage nodded. "Taken care of." Even if he explained the procedure he'd used, what he'd done, Grier wouldn't get it. He'd happily leave the computer shit to Sage. And he'd trust him to have his back. The fact Sage had kept Mia's association with the Omens from him didn't matter now.

The plan was simple. They were storming the place. No real finesse, just breaking down doors, shooting anyone who wasn't Fiona or London. Demons had been called in from every chapter up and down the coast, and the building was surrounded, men waiting for the go-sign from Grier.

"You ready?" Sage nudged Grier, and he nodded, gave the sign and waited for it to travel around the building. It was time and one way or another, this would end tonight.

Glass broke and the first shots echoed through the quiet of the night. Grier waited for the back door to fly open. When it crashed and splintered into shards of wood, Grier burst inside. His men were everywhere. In doorways, the hall, pushing open doors, gathering up the Omens and their women.

He pushed past Hamilton, shoving doors open, checking rooms already checked. "Where is she?" He couldn't stem the panic. His gut ached and his eyes blurred. She had to be there somewhere. The last door he opened had only a set of steps that led down. He didn't wait for back-up. He couldn't. Fiona was there somewhere, and he could feel it. The steps creaked and moaned, seemed to stretch endlessly into the darkness, but he moved quickly as if he wasn't shaking from adrenaline and fear.

No sound. No light. Just a hallway. More doors. He tried one, shined the light from his phone inside. Empty but for a few stacks of chairs. The next room and the one after that were more of the same. He tried another.

"Come in. I've been expecting you."

Fiona, recognizable by only her hair and what he could see of her eyes, stood in front of an old man who had a knife to her throat. London sat on the floor off to the side by a refrigerator.

Grier raised his gun and aimed at his father's forehead. One inch off the mark and Fiona would die but Grier didn't waver. Someone was going to die today, and it wouldn't be his wife or daughter, that much he knew for sure.

GRIER COULD SEE three moves ahead. Sedotal would come in behind him. Carr would play his card with Fiona as the ante, but he couldn't kill her, which meant they would go after London. He put his body between Carr and the baby. There would only be time for one shot. Grier moved away from the door, further into the room and a calm settled over him. He pulled a second gun from his waistband at his back and aimed it at Sedotal who'd walked in behind him and pushed the door shut.

"And here we all are." With his arms straight out, Grier shook his head. "All these years. You could've called."

"And miss all this fun." Sedotal aimed at Fiona. "I'd put that down if I was you. If you shoot me, I shoot her, and dear old dad shoots you. Poor baby is an orphan and we both know what happens to orphans, don't we, Grier?"

Sedotal knew shit. Or maybe he did, but Grier couldn't see, didn't care about anything but Fiona, the bruises on her face, the knife at her throat, the hate in her eyes.

He looked at Sedotal. Carr didn't have a gun and Grier didn't bother pointing out the flaw in his logic. With or without the threat of a stray bullet from Carr, the variables weren't in Grier's favor. But no way could he lower either gun.

Carr looked at Sedotal then Grier, smirk twisted, eyes bloodshot. "How's your mother?"

Grier shrugged. "Dead."

The smirk fell. Fiona gasped. Sedotal tensed. And still, Grier's calm remained.

"How?" Carr's voice faltered until it was almost a groan.

All along, Grier had thought Carr killed Jez. But it must've been Sedotal. That Carr didn't know it could work to his favor, at least until Carr pushed the knife hard enough into Fiona's throat that a bloom of red appeared, and a small line of blood trailed down to her collarbone.

"I thought maybe you could tell me, but I guess I've been blaming the wrong guy." He shrugged again. "Must've been him." He jerked the gun toward Sedotal. Goddammit. He should've known it was Sedotal. A death like the one Jez endured had Sedotal's prints all over it.

Carr stared at Sedotal. "You?"

Sedotal stared at his father. "She… I had to." Carr pushed Fiona aside so that she landed on the floor. Then he lunged at Sedotal, knife poised to strike. Sedotal fired at the same moment Carr thrust the knife into his son's neck. Fiona crawled toward the baby and Grier caught Carr as Sedotal shoved him away. Sedotal made for the door as Grier laid his father on the ground. Torn between staying with Fiona and catching that bastard, he looked down at his father and blocked all emotion. This was the same man who'd beaten his mother badly enough she'd had no choice but to hide him away in a foster care system where he was beaten and abused. In this moment, he couldn't let anything in. Fiona needed him strong. Decisive. Ready to kill for her.

Fiona stayed by the baby, huddled in on herself, her body surrounding the baby's chair as if to shield London from the ugliness in the room.

Grier shoved his Glock into his waistband and slid the other gun across the floor to Fiona.

She glanced up and spoke through gritted teeth. "Get Sedotal and kill that bastard!"

Grier ran from the room and before he reached the parking lot, he heard the shot and knew what Fiona had done. God, what they must've put her through. He watched Sedotal speed down the street and climbed onto a bike that belonged to one of the Omens. A BMW tricked out with a speedometer that went to 210 and by God, if he needed to, he'd push it that far.

He took off, through the back gate, weaving in and out of traffic, knowing if Sedotal got away he might never find him. Sedotal took a left. Grier followed. He weaved around a car and into the path of a truck, quickly back to his own side of the road and Grier stayed close.

The tracks ahead, with a train stopped over the crossing, gates down, wouldn't stop either of them. Grier knew Sedotal's next move and planned his. There would be a turn. A right toward the harbor, parallel to the tracks, between the train and the old rail yard where they kept the no longer used cabooses and empty cars. He would stay between them until he could cross into the shipyard at the harbor and try to lose Grier in the maze of trailers and freight. He was back to seeing three moves ahead and it made that same calm feeling settle in, gave him the confidence to speed up.

But Sedotal made the left, not the right. Took them toward the city, the alleys and side roads that would allow him cover and make killing him without risking other lives impossible. He pictured Fiona, broken, bruised, probably more damaged mentally than physically. The calm vanished and the rage surfaced, pushed Grier to a point of not giving a fuck about collateral damage. Sedotal would pay. Every Omen he found would die for what happened to her. He raced ahead and Sedotal turned onto a side road then again into an alley, wound between two buildings. He slid to a stop at the fence ending the throughway and whipped the bike around, aimed and shot. Could've been blood loss or just that the fucker had bad aim, but the bullet ricocheted off the brick building.

Grier wasn't Evel Knievel. Wasn't a stunt man. Wasn't ready to die. He revved the bike again and took off. One of them was going to end up in hell. Now.

11

God bless morphine and the painless bliss it gave Fiona. Three days worth of feeling nothing. And three days since she'd seen Grier. Hamilton, on the other hand, hadn't left her side. They'd had to change London over to formula. She vaguely remembered hearing someone say that to her, vaguely remembered Hamilton helping her hold the baby. Everything was vague. Hazy.

She blinked her eyes. So dry. Tried to lift her head. Too heavy. With the drug, she felt weightless. Without them, she couldn't move. And everything ached. No, not ached. Agonized. Tortured. Worse than the beatings.

"Ham." She had said it. She was sure. But no sound came. "Ham." She was screaming but still no sound. "Hamilton!" A tear slipped down her cheek and she tried to lift her hand to wipe it away but no matter how hard she concentrated, she couldn't move. "Ham! Ham! Help me!"

He sat in the chair next to her bed watching the TV. Jesus. Was she even blinking? Was she alive?

She tried again to move, tried again to lift her arm. Her head. A foot. And nothing. Her fingers fluttered, wrapped around the lower rail on the side of her bed. She loosened them then gripped again, trying to make a noise so Hamilton would look at her, see her.

She breathed out as hard as she could. She tried for a wheeze or a whimper or a cry, but nothing came.

She closed her eyes but could see everything, every light, every machine hooked to her body. She could see London in a small bed by Hamilton. A nurse at the desk across from her open door. A window with moonlight streaming through. And she knew it had been three days because... she just knew.

The picture of her father sat beside the bed in her room. A picture of Grier next to it.

She was lying on her own pillow. In her own room. There wasn't a rail, but a pillow supporting her broken hand.

"Ham." There. A whisper. And he looked at her.

"Shit. Fiona." He put his hand on her forehead. Even that gentle touch echoed through the cavern inside her skull. For such a big man his tears were normal size.

"Grier?"

"He... he's... in jail."

"Sedotal?" Every word cost her.

"In the wind. Cops got called for the shots. They got Grier on a gun charge. They found him with a Glock and a bike stolen out of Vermont." He brushed her hair off her forehead. "His friend's girl is coming to help. Don't worry. Then you're all getting out. He's taking you somewhere safe."

"Safe?" She couldn't process. Jail. Gun charge. Vermont. Friend's girl. She had to take it down to small phrases. Work her way through them one by one.

Jail. Simple enough. Gun charge. Hmph. Remarkably, he'd never been in jail, after all these years. She didn't know what Vermont had to do with anything. Friend's girl. Oh shit. Not her. No. No. No.

Fiona tried to shake her head but couldn't move her neck. Now, she lifted her not broken hand which worked just fine, brought it to her throat. Heavy bandage.

"It's gone, Fi. The leg, too."

She teared up again. "Thank you."

"Doctor Foley."

Ah. Dr. Foley. Max's friend, Elliot. He was one of those guys who was convinced he was a god. Fancy car. Wife young enough to be his late in life daughter. A retirement plan fit for a king. Most of it from the

Demons. And maybe… it was right on the tip of her tongue. Something she needed to realize.

Dammit.

What was it? She closed her eyes. Had said maybe ten words. Maybe not even and it made her eyes heavy. But she needed to think… later.

* * *

Fiona woke again. Tried her voice. "Ham?"

"I'm here." He laid a hand over hers.

"Get Foley." It came to her as soon as she opened her eyes. Foley wasn't just a doctor. He was a doctor who pandered to those who paid the most. And last she'd seen Tyler Sedotal, he'd had the hilt of a knife sticking out of his neck.

"I'm not leaving you."

"Then get someone else to get Foley." She still couldn't move her jaw, but everything else seemed to be waking up. And she was smart enough to know having Hamilton in the room was the safest she'd ever be. He went to the door and called for Sage, relayed the message and came back to stand beside her bed. "Eliana will be here soon." He glanced down and his tongue clicked his teeth. "Any instructions?"

"If she doesn't get Grier out, kill her." Oh, yeah. Years

and years of bad blood still existed. Max might have erased the debt, not that Fiona knew for sure, but that didn't mean Fiona forgave it. Also, it didn't matter that Eliana's debt technically belonged to her old man, the father, not Kye. Kye had been a leader once, the man Max had planned to leave the club to. Then she came along. And Kye had turned, run out on the club, stabbed Max, killed more than one Demon. All because he liked fucking her more than he respected his place in the club. Worse, he'd taken Grier with him. They had some soul-mate, kindred brotherhood shit Fiona didn't under-stand. didn't care to understand. But now, Eliana was useful. Maybe. If not, the old debt would come due. Period.

She stared at Hamilton. "Tell me about Jez." She needed to feed her anger, keep it strong because the emotions were coming back and whatever was under-neath the anger would kill her. Knowing what happened to Jez would help.

"Fi…" Hamilton shook his head.

It probably wasn't fair to use his feeling for her against him, but she needed to know. "Please?" She summoned a tear, a skill she'd acquired at an early age, one that had seen her through her teen years, earned her a Beemer, a bike of her own, the house she lived in, and Grier. "Ham, please." She curled her fingers around his.

He closed his eyes and breathed out. "They took her

from her house. We found her at the old compound. She was beaten and stabbed and already gone by the time we found her."

"It was Sedotal." Not exactly a newsflash.

"Yeah." Hamilton nodded. He looked down, swallowed hard, and sniffed. "Did they... did they touch you?"

More than half beating her to death? Holding her down and branding her? Staring while she fed London. All things considered, it could've been worse. But she knew what he meant. "No."

She pictured Jez. Tough. Like a mother to Fiona over the years. She'd been one of Max's best friends. A member of the club since the beginning. And now she was gone. And the man responsible was walking around breathing and eating and living. That had to stop.

The key would be Foley. Her gut said so. If he didn't know where Sedotal was, he would know someone who did. And when they found him... she would've smiled if it didn't hurt so bad. Instead, she laid in the bed, plotting his death, the pictures in her head of what she planned to do to him providing a sense of peace that let her drift back to sleep, content and happy.

"SIGN HERE." Eliana stood next to Grier as the guard handed him a bag of his stuff—wallet, keys, seventy-eight cents in change. They were keeping the Glock. Dammit.

Jail hadn't been so bad. Of course, it was no walk in the park, but he'd gathered some intel on Sedotal. The Omens had men posted along the entire east coast and their usual base of operations was in Florida. They'd come north when the Screaming Demons got out of the human trafficking business, when Max died and Fiona took over. The Omens, Tyler specifically, weren't looking to take over the Demon drug trade or the illegal parts trade, they wanted Max's contacts for the women, the "supplier".

Not that it mattered. All that mattered was that Fiona was home, safe, recovering. But until Sedotal and his crew were off the streets, Fiona and London would be in danger, and no damned way was he going to let anything happen to them again.

"Is Kye happy in Belize?" He walked beside Eli to the desk out front.

She smiled. "I like to think so." She shrugged. "He misses riding his bike, misses his friends, but you know... I try to keep him busy."

When they'd run off to Belize, Grier had enjoyed surfing. He had enjoyed the sun and sand and lazy days with no one threatening to shoot him or the people he loved. Back then, he hadn't realized how important that would be.

Eli shook her head. "She's never going to be happy there. This is her life. This is who she was born to be."

When Grier closed his eyes, he saw the brand on her neck, the misshapen cheeks and the purple bruises. Right now, Fiona's happiness wasn't nearly as important as her safety.

"I can't keep her safe here." Truth told, he was tired of dealing with everything, of knowing everything he knew. He wanted out, and he wanted Fiona with him.

"Can you promise she won't try to kill me in my sleep?"

Grier smiled as they waited for the guard to press the button that would open the door to the outside. "Probably... not, but maybe I can keep her busy enough she doesn't think about it."

It felt good to breathe air not tainted by BO and piss and Grier took an extra-long inhale and let it out slowly as the door swung open and he and Eli walked out into the sunlight. Maybe he should've gone straight to the streets to hunt down Sedotal, but all he wanted was to go home, wrap his arms around Fiona and hold her and the baby.

He blew through stoplights, took a couple of corners fast enough Eli hung onto the door handle with both hands, and finally pulled the car in front of their house.

"Grier, wait." Eli grabbed his arm as he popped open the door. "She's been through a lot."

Yeah. A lot. Too much for Grier to think about and not put his fist through a wall. He nodded.

"What I'm saying is, go easy. Follow her lead, okay?"

"I will." She opened her door and met him at the front of the car. "You coming in?"

Eli shook her head. "I'm going back to the hotel. I don't think I'm exactly what's going to make Fiona feel better right now."

He nodded, not because he agreed but because he wanted to end this conversation and get inside. "Thanks for getting me out."

"I'll get everything arranged and we'll talk this evening."

He nodded and tried not to run up the walk. Technically, jogging wasn't running.

He didn't stop to say hi to any of the guys in the living room. Didn't go to the fridge for food. Didn't even worry about taking a leak. Instead, he raced to the bedroom.

Hamilton looked up and nodded at him as Grier stood in the doorway. The bruises on Fiona's face were not so purple now but a sick shade of green and yellow and she had a bandage on the left side of her throat. But she'd never looked so good to him. His throat closed behind a lump and his eyes burned with tears threatening to leak down his face. He bypassed Hamilton and went to the bed, slipped beneath the blankets and wrapped his arms around Fiona. She flinched but turned toward him, laid her arm over his side and buried her face in the curve of his shoulder.

Her shoulders shook and he tightened his hold around her as Hamilton nodded and left them alone.

He stroked her hair, felt the line of stitches near the crown of her head and whispered as she cried. The words didn't matter. Holding Fiona mattered.

When the tears subsided and her breathing leveled to normal, Grier pulled back to look at her and she tilted her chin down. "Hey." He curled his finger and used it to urge her face back up.

"I don't…" Her voice caught. "I don't want you to see me like this."

He brushed a finger over her eyebrow. The bruises didn't matter to him. The swelling would go down and the color would fade. Even if it didn't, he wouldn't care. "You're beautiful, Fiona." He kissed the spot on her cheek where her skin had been scraped off. Then her swollen jaw, then the corner of her lower lip where it had been busted open. "Nothing they did changed that." He pushed her hair back. "I'm sorry I wasn't here for you and that I didn't find you in time." His voice broke every time he talked or thought about what they'd done to her. What kind of husband let his wife go through that?

"I want to get out of here."

"Okay." He would have walked through fire for her, and if she wanted to go out, there were plenty of guys here that would be look-outs so they could enjoy the night. "Where should we go? There's a new Italian place one of the guards told me about."

She shook her head. "I mean away from all of this. Out of this town. No more business. Just us. Safe. With London." She looked up at him and her tears almost broke him.

"We can do whatever you want." There was an entire world they could explore together.

"Kye said we could come to Belize." She smiled. "You can teach the baby to surf. I can learn how to make grass skirts or something. We can be… safe."

Oh, God. That sounded so good. But Eliana's words, she was born for this, echoed in his head. Making grass skirts would never be enough for Fiona, even if she couldn't see it now.

She snuggled closer. "We could spend every day in bed. Make London a little brother or sister."

Now, this was an idea he could get behind. But he didn't want her to have regrets. "I would love that." He kissed the top of her head. There would never be a time he got tired of holding her. "How about we nap on it?

And if you still want to go when we wake up, we'll pack up. Okay?"

He would take her anywhere in the world she wanted to go, but he had to make sure leaving was really what she wanted. Not that they couldn't come back, but once they left, everything would change and coming back might end up being harder than walking away.

12

Fiona stared out of the window at the ocean. They'd been in Belize for almost two weeks and she needed... something. Some sign her husband didn't consider her damaged goods, something to ease the anxiety. Sex with Grier, that was what she needed. In the dark. Because while Foley had done a rather remarkable job on removing the brand on her throat, the scar on the inside of her thigh looked remarkably still like Tyler's initials. And she couldn't stand the sight. Didn't expect it would enhance what she needed to be a mind-altering experience.

He'd gone fishing with Kye, and Fiona was starving, but though Eli had been so kind since they'd been in Belize, Fiona didn't want to run into her. After everything that had happened, Eli would probably understand Fiona threatening her life if she didn't free Grier from jail, but it wasn't a moment Fiona was proud of. And the shame reared its head every time they ran into each other in the hall or the kitchen.

Like now, for example. Eli walked into the kitchen. She stopped at the refrigerator and pulled out a pitcher of juice, and the cabinet for a couple of glasses then went to the table behind Fiona.

"You look better."

Oh yeah. The bruises had faded. The swelling went down.

Fiona nodded. "Yeah." For all the good it did her. The nightmares hadn't gone anywhere. She'd shot William Carr in cold blood, worn the blowback of his brain matter.

Eli poured the glasses of juice. "I didn't know what my dad did."

So, it was a heart to heart she wanted. Fiona grinned. "Well, that's lucky because I knew everything my dad did." And she'd done nothing to stop him, enjoyed the rewards of his lawlessness, ignored the people who went missing from her life and those who showed up to replace them. Now, she'd turned into him. Her stomach quivered at the thought, and she blew out a long breath.

"Sit." She slid a glass along the surface of the table. The grinding of glass against wood made Fiona cringe but she turned from the window and sat across from Eliana. "We aren't the sins of our parents."

Maybe Eli wasn't. But Fiona had only added to the Strong family quotient for evil. "I told Ham to kill you if you couldn't get Grier out of jail."

"I know." Eli smiled. "Do you think I wouldn't kill for Kye?" Little Eliana what's-her-name a killer? Laughable. "He's alive now because of you. I'm alive now because of him. Actually, we both are. And Grier." She smiled. "It's family. It's what your family does."

Was this bitch implying they were family? "My family kills. It's what we do." She sighed. Oh, dear God, the truth made her stomach ache. "It's what I do."

"I think you did what you needed to do." She smiled cryptically. "Funny, isn't it? What we'll do to protect the people we love?"

Fiona stared at the juice in front of her. "Without the club and the clothes and the guys, I don't know who I am." So, heart to heart, after all. "I don't know if I'm enough."

"For him?" Eliana chuckled. "You're everything to Grier."

Then why was he pretending to sleep with her, sneaking out after he thought she fell asleep, coming back just before dawn? "I think you overestimate his devotion."

"And I think you underestimate it." She cocked an eyebrow. "Maybe try to reconnect. You've been through something horrible. But you're not alone. He's… yours. No matter what."

But what did Fiona have to offer him in return? And she didn't have time to think about it. He walked in the back door with Kye.

Eli leaned in. "He thinks you need time. He won't know what to do unless you tell him." Then she sat up and smiled at Kye. "What do you say we take the kids today and…" She chewed her lower lip then tilted her head. "Practice having two?"

Kye's eyebrows pinched toward his nose. "Do we need to practice having two?"

"Not yet." She stood and wrapped her arms around him. "But never hurts to be prepared."

Kye kissed the tip of her nose. "My little Boy Scout."

Grier stood just inside the door and Fiona ignored anything else Kye and Eliana said. He didn't look at her, didn't look at Kye and Eli, didn't seem to be seeing anything. And that was what Fiona needed to change.

It took an hour to get the babies ready, diaper bags packed, bottles made, strollers unfolded, and babies secured inside. Then Fiona and Grier were alone.

He'd decided on a shower, alone, and Fiona waited all of three minutes. She couldn't take anymore waiting, anymore planning her seduction. Instead, she stripped off her clothes, took a deep breath and walked into the bathroom.

He used to sing in the shower, Bon Jovi or Springsteen. His rendition of "Born in the USA" always made her smile. He didn't sing anymore.

She steamrolled through the bathroom and she waved it away enough to see the glass shower door, to see her husband standing with his head bowed under the water.

She didn't speak, didn't breathe until she opened the door and stepped in behind him, touched his shoulder, and he turned. "Hello."

"I thought maybe you could use a… hand?" She wrapped her fingers around his cock, smiled at his quiet moan. "I miss you."

He lowered his head and brushed his lips over hers then drew away and came back in to deliver a kiss that rocked her, that stole her ability to think or do more than feel.

When he tore his mouth away and held her back with his hand on her shoulder, she closed her eyes and let go of him.

She couldn't tell if it was the water or tears, but she shook her head.

"I don't know what to do, Fiona. I don't want to hurt you."

"Hurt me?" He was killing her.

"We haven't talked about what happened. What they… did to you."

Oh enough. The eggshell walking. The silent looks between Grier and his friends none of them thought she saw. The way he pretended to still love her. E-fucking-nough.

She pushed him against the wall. "I don't need to talk or to rehash what happened. I need you to fuck me. Right now." He didn't move, didn't try to fight her. Even kissed her back when she crushed his mouth with hers, wrapped her in his arms. But nothing more.

It didn't take a genius to figure it out. He was giving her the power back. Not that she'd lost it. She hadn't wavered, hadn't lost anything she needed to survive.

She kissed him again. Harder. More desperate. Worked his dick until he groaned and slapped his hand flat against the wall and panted.

"Tell me what you want, Fiona."

Ah. There he was.

She lifted his hand and put it on her breast. Oh, God. He rolled her nipple between his fingers and her body went weak. She'd missed him. With his free hand, he lifted her knee to his hip and held it, pumping his cock into her hand. "Put me inside you." he lowered his head and took her breast in his mouth, teased and soothed, sucked and kissed.

From that moment on, she lost herself in Grier.

* * *

FINALLY. He'd spent weeks dreaming of being inside her again, of feeling her against him, hearing her soft moans, watching her eyelids flutter when she was close to letting go. And for weeks, he'd held back, gave her space. And it almost killed him.

Now, he was so close, ready to plunge his dick inside her and he couldn't. He couldn't risk hurting her.

"Come on, baby." She stroked him, pulling and squeezing his cock until he couldn't think rationally, didn't want to remember she'd been through something horrible and needed the soft, sweetness of making love rather than the frenzy of fucking.

He needed to make this about her, slow it down, worship her to counteract the horrors they'd inflicted on her.

"Fiona." He kissed her neck, her nipple, her stomach, and finally knelt in front of her and pushed her leg up to rest on his shoulder. She threw her head back and cried out and he kissed her clit, then licked and sucked until she threaded her fingers through his hair and screamed his name.

When her trembling stopped, he moved back and for the first time, he saw it, the puckered flesh on her thigh. Another brand.

Fuck. He closed his eyes and she covered the spot with her hand. "Don't look." Her breath hitched and her shoulders shook.

Oh, God. What she'd gone through. And he hadn't saved her from any of it. Fuck!

He stood and pulled her close, shut the water off and wrapped them in a towel while she continued crying.

"Hey." But she shook her head. So, he held her until they were both dry then he dropped the towel and swung her into his arms. Rage burned through him along with a need to avenge the wrongs perpetrated on his wife. His wife. But right now, she needed him. And by God, he wouldn't let her down again.

He laid her on the bed and slid under the blankets beside her.

He'd missed her skin, the silky feel of it, the slightly sweet taste, the scent that belonged to just her. "Please, Grier." She rubbed her body against his and it didn't take a genius to know what she was asking.

Need and want mingled in his gut, and he kissed her, soft at first, slow and deep. His body throbbed with desire and she ground her hips against his cock and a whimper vibrated in her throat.

Grier wanted to go slow, to caress every inch of her, but Fiona shoved him onto his back and rolled until she was on top, then sat up to lower herself onto his dick, taking him one slow inch at a time, teasing him with her slick wet pussy and those fingertips, tweaking his nipples, sliding down his gut, to touch herself.

So hot. So fucking perfect. She arched her back, set

the rhythm, slow and seductive, and waited until he was so close to shooting a load inside her before she called out his name and moved with such urgency he exploded.

When she collapsed onto his chest, chest heaving, body trembling, Grier kissed the top of her head and squeezed her closer. "I love you." Maybe she wasn't ready to hear the words, but he needed to say them.

And he tried not to be hurt that she didn't say it back to him. Instead, he tilted her chin up for a kiss. But now that he wasn't inside her anymore and his thoughts cleared, the fury came back, roared through his blood. They'd branded her. Twice. Branded. Like property.

His body tensed. And Fiona noticed, lifted her head. "Hey."

Grier couldn't speak, couldn't even look at her. He'd failed her. His fault. His fault. His fault. He should've been on that plane with her instead of playing outlaw with a motorcycle club that he'd led into trap after trap. And they'd branded her.

"I'm so sorry." His voice broke and tears leaked down his cheeks. He was lying next to her crying like a baby, letting her console him. It took a minute before he could speak. "I'm going to kill that son of a bitch."

She smoothed his hair back. "It's done with. I'm fine and London is fine and we're safe now."

Her words registered on his too-late-for-words level. She'd be safe for the rest of her life and he'd make sure.

"I'm going back and I'm going to find him." And burn him alive.

"No." She shook her head. "You can't. It's not safe." Her defeated sigh shook him. "Let the club handle him. Let them worry. We have this now. A place he can't get to us. We have each other."

"Fiona."

She pushed him off and sat up. "When he had me, all I could think about was getting back to you, being safe with you. It—you got me through that. I don't need him dead." She cupped Grier's cheek. "I thought I did, but then I saw you and knew I didn't need anything but you. I can survive what happened, but I won't survive losing you."

The words should have calmed his rage, but only inflamed him further. "And you think he'll get to me first?" Of course she did. Why wouldn't she? Nothing he'd done would have convinced her otherwise, but this wasn't about the club. This was about his family, the only one he'd ever had outside of Kye.

"No. But he's unpredictable, and I don't want to take a chance on a stray bullet or... anything else. You're mine now, and I want to keep what's mine close to me."

Goddammit. The wet-lashed plea. The silent don't-let-me-down look. The irresistible weapons she had in her arsenal. "Fiona, as long as he's out there, this is your prison. You'll never be safe outside of these gates. And maybe not inside. London will never be safe. I have to go. This has to end so we can live our lives."

"Do I look unhappy here? This was my idea. My picket fence, Grier. I don't give a damn about going back to Pine Hill. There's nothing there for us."

Max would be rolling in his grave if he heard her now. He'd left her everything he had, everything he'd built, and Grier had ruined it for her. Made her not want it. Destroyed everything. Fuck.

"Fiona, I have to go back. We won't have peace anywhere until we don't have to worry about him anymore, until we don't have to look over our shoulders." The threat would remain as long as Sedotal was breathing and Grier refused to let his family live that way.

She sighed. "If you go, I'm going with you."

The hell she was. "No. Out of the question." He was protecting her, not throwing her back into the fray. And there would be a fray. Besides, she didn't want to go. A deaf man would have heard the fear and doubt in her voice.

"Then what am I supposed to do? Sit here on my hands while you're back there playing superhero?" She shook her head. "That's not going to happen."

"You shot him. Carr stabbed him. And I'm going to

finish him. It's my turn. He's a threat to my family, to the two people I love more than anything in the world." Maybe if he softened his words, used his love for her, she would understand why it had to be him and him alone. If not, if she couldn't go along with it, maybe she could look back on this moment later and forgive him because he was doing this for them. For their family. "I don't want to live our lives without peace. Without knowing I did everything I could to protect you and London. Please try to… understand."

She leaned forward and laid her head on his chest. "Promise you'll come back to me."

"I promise." He would kill Sedotal and then they could restart their lives together.

13

Fiona watched Grier. When he slept. While he was awake. In the shower. On the beach. Everywhere he went, she kept watch, unable to stand the thought of not seeing him. His hair had the same streaks of white-blond he'd had a year ago, and his skin had a sun-kissed glow to it.

And she was about to let him go back to Pine Hill. Alone. To fight a guy who didn't fight fair. And if she lost Grier…

Fiona took her cup of coffee to the veranda and watched Grier sitting on the beach staring out at the water. How was she supposed to let him go back? Let him walk into danger?

Kye opened the door and looked out. "Oh, sorry."

Maybe he could help her convince Grier not to go. "No, please." She gestured to a chair and smiled when he sat, coffee in hand, hair tousled as if he'd just come from bed. They'd talked, overcome the past, for Grier's sake and because Kye was genuinely good, concerned for her family enough to offer his home to protect them.

She waited and watched Grier. "He's going back."

Kye nodded. "I know. He told me." He drank his cup of juice like his friend wasn't heading off to start a war with a heavily armed asshole and the asshole's entire crew.

"Can you talk to him? Tell him there's no reason to leave here and going back is gonna get him killed?" Fiona had tried everything else—tears, begging, sex, begging during sex—and still, she couldn't persuade him.

All her life, until Grier anyway, she'd managed to avoid bikers, especially ones who belonged to a club. She'd seen what their loyalty did to relationships. Plus, Max wanted her out of the business, only left it to her as a last resort, and she knew it, despite everything he'd said to her and everyone else. Back then she'd picked her dates from the other side of the tracks, the side where there weren't drive-by shootings and a death a day. All the while making Grier follow her around because he'd been the one she'd always wanted. She'd broken all the rules she'd set for herself and now she was paying for it.

Kye shook his head. "It would be crazy for me to talk him out of it." He grinned. "I hate traveling alone."

There was some consolation that Kye was going with him, but not enough to calm the anxious energy that kept her foot tapping and her hands shaking every minute since Grier had decided he was leaving.

"Is there anything I can say that will make him stay?"

Kye shook his head. "Tyler Sedotal took something from Grier that Grier has to go get back. It isn't pride or money or the usual. He took Grier's security and his peace of mind. That's not something we can give him. He has to end this thing because more than he wants to, he needs to."

Fiona shook her head. "Isn't it enough that me and the baby are alive and with him?" More than anything she wanted to know why it *wasn't* enough, but she couldn't ask. Instead, she closed her eyes, cursed Grier for being the man she'd always known he was, a good man who wouldn't let anyone hurt his family and get away with it. Damn it.

Kye stared at her. "I'm guessing right about now you're realizing why you married him, why he's the guy. And he's out there—" he pointed to Grier still sitting in the sand, "—thinking he has to give you up to be the man we both know he needs to be."

Fiona shook her head, stood and walked to the edge

of the concrete before she turned back to him. "I never liked you, you big know it all."

He grinned and Fiona understood the attraction Eli had to him. "Yeah, I know. That's okay. We both love him and that's enough." He chuckled. "Go out there and be who he needs right now." He held up the baby monitor. "I'll listen for London."

She thought about telling him how to mix the formula and where she kept the diapers, but he had a kid. He could figure that out himself. Instead, she walked out onto the beach toward Grier and didn't stop until she was close enough to see the streaks of blond in his hair, the slump of his shoulders, the curl of his fingers in the sand.

She knelt beside him and put her hand on his shoulder. "Working on your tan?"

He turned and sighed. "I love you so much, but I have to do this."

Oh, God. Why did he have to be so… everything to her? "I know."

"It doesn't mean…" She cut him off with a kiss, and when he pulled back, he smiled.

"Come with me." She stood and held out her hand. There was a place she'd found, a cove with crystal water and high rocks, a place where she could at least make a memory with him that she could cherish. Just in case.

"What about London?" But he stood and threaded his fingers through hers.

"Kye's taking care of her." She led him down the beach, away from the house. She didn't have words to let him know that she understood his need to go. Showing him was all she could do.

"You know, growing up, I had a huge crush on you."

He chuckled and brought her hand to his mouth and kissed her knuckles. "I seem to recall Brad Pitt's picture hanging on your bedroom wall."

"Can you imagine what Max would've done if he had walked in my room and found a life-sized picture of you hanging on my wall?" She clicked her tongue. Max would have had Grier taken and castrated. "Back then… if you would've just smiled at me just once…" She sighed.

"I'm smiling at you now."

Oh yeah, he was. And her heart fluttered in that same old way it always had. "Better than all those fantasies I used to have."

He turned to face her and pulled her in close. "You must tell me about these fantasies you speak of. I'm intrigued." He kissed the curve where her shoulder met her throat. She shivered and ran her hand over his chest, his warm, broad chest.

"The reality of you is so much better than the fantasy." And wasn't that just the damned truth of it? On one hand, she hated herself for loving him, for loving a man at all when it could destroy her now to lose him. On the other hand, she finally understood what loving him meant. "I know you have to go, but can we just have today to pretend you don't?" No. She wouldn't cry, not today. She would save it for later, when he couldn't see. "Maybe you could teach me to surf?"

He smiled. "Can't surf here. The reef…"

He didn't finish because she couldn't let him. She needed to kiss him, to feel him inside her. And damned if she wanted to wait another minute.

THE ONLY THING that distracted Grier from his rage and fury was Fiona. Holding her. Kissing her. Loving her. Otherwise, the anger vibrated through him, so out of control he could hardly contain it or breathe through it. Only Fiona quieted that beast.

And he needed her now, her body against his, her soft sighs in his ear, the surrender between them. Her eyes, half-lidded and sparkling with desire, closed when he ran his finger along her jaw. She tilted her head back, exposing a long line of skin and bringing their lower bodies closer, so close. "Swim with me?"

He almost swallowed his tongue. "You want to swim now?" Not at all what he had in mind until she stepped back and stripped off her shirt, then stepped out of her shorts and walked toward the water. She didn't mean swim at all, the little vixen. And thank God for it.

When she reached the edge where the water met a drop-off, she dove in and Grier waited until she surfaced before he even blinked. Before he *could* even blink.

"You coming in?"

Oh, yeah. God, yeah. It would take an army to keep him out. He walked toward the water, shedding the few articles of clothing he wore, then dove in. The water was warm, like silk along his skin. Or he'd thought so until he pulled Fiona close. *She* felt like silk. After she kissed him until he couldn't think straight, she swam away, turned and crooked a finger. "Come on." She led him to the other side of the cove where the sun shined on a formation of smooth flat rocks. She climbed out of the water and laid back on the one closest to them, supporting herself on her elbows. He'd never seen anything so beautiful in his life. If it killed him, he would make sure no one ever hurt her again. But first...

He pulled himself up next to her, the sun warm and irrelevant. The wind cool and unimportant. Nothing but this moment with Fiona mattered.

"I love you." He lowered his head and kissed her, soft at first, slow, then desperate and frenzied. His hand skimmed over her rib cage, down to curl into her hip and urge her on top of him. He needed too much, wanted too much, and she would get hurt if he left her with her back against the rock.

She guided his hands, captured his mouth, joined them and moved slowly, each slide down his cock as agonizing as it was perfect, until he couldn't do more than move his hips and moan.

When he let go, she came with him, held on to him as tightly as he held her. Before his world settled, she rolled away and laid her hand over her stomach. "I know you have to go."

He nodded, not really wanting to start round two of their argument just yet.

"Just make sure you come back to me, okay?" Her voice cracked but she held her head up, tears glittering in her eyes.

"I promise." Grier couldn't move. He didn't want to. If these were the last minutes they were to have in God knew how long, he didn't want to waste even one of them. He stretched beside her and leaned in.

* * *

FIONA CHUCKLED, but not one damned thing about this was funny. How he'd managed to get a sunburn on his ass on a day he had to sit on a plane for hours and hours was beyond comprehension. Not really since he'd spent a good number of hours with his ass exposed to direct sunlight while he used his body to love Fiona.

"Can you please just rub the aloe on me? Please?" He glared over his shoulder as her lips twitched. "Fiona?"

"Of course."

Maybe having her hands on his butt wasn't such a fine idea. Wasn't that how this got started in the first place?

Her touch, so soft and tentative made him want to turn and… no. The last thing he needed was an untimely boner. Absolutely no time for this. He had a flight to catch. A brother to kill. Sunburns and sex did not fit into the schedule, but his body didn't give a shit about timelines or funeral planning. It liked her hands smoothing that gel on his skin. It loved the skim of her fingers, needed more.

But then his brain forced all his doubts to the front. Had she manipulated him into all that sex to keep him here, to make sure he missed his flight?

His stomach clenched and he turned to face her. "You're pretty smart, aren't you?"

She sat back and wiped her hands on a towel. "I like to think so. In general, yeah." She quirked an eyebrow. "We aren't talking generalities, are we?"

So cool and collected. But she didn't understand, and for once her touch, her soft voice, even the love he felt for her couldn't overcome his fury. "You did this, didn't you?" He pointed to his ass.

She scoffed. "Doggie style, and by the way, I hate that you call it that, was all your idea, Einstein. All three times. In a cove. By crystal clear water that acts like a mirror to reflect the sun." Her own brand of anger flashed in her eyes and across the tight line of her mouth.

He'd just wanted her so bad. And now, if he didn't make this right, which he didn't have time for, their last words before he left would be angry.

"I'm sorry." He turned on his side to face her and reached to twirl a strand of coppery hair around his finger. "I know you weren't trying to distract me from leaving."

She chuckled again and shook her head. "You are… not so smart. I was trying to distract you, but I knew it wouldn't work. I had a good time trying though." She clicked her tongue against her teeth and winked. "The sunburn maybe is some… karmic justice for leaving me here without you. But totally your own fault."

He nodded and stood to pull up his jeans. The scratch of cotton and denim against his skin felt like sandpaper and he flinched. "Not fun."

She grinned. "Justice." When she turned away, she took a long breath.

He had to make this better. "Every time I sit or move,

I'm gonna remember this day." The whole thing. The smiles, the touching, the talking and loving. "I love you, Fiona." He tangled his fingers in her hair and tugged until their breaths mingled and she leaned her forehead against his chest.

"I love you, too."

It had been weeks since he'd heard her say it. Months maybe. And his heart did a little dance behind his ribcage.

Leaving her to make sure they were safe made sense on every level except the one where his heart lived. And that was another thing Tyler Sedotal would pay for. From here on, Grier would keep track of every minute he was away from Fiona and London and add them to Sedotal's tab. And by the time he was finished killing him, there wouldn't be anything left to be found.

Fiona slept alone. Woke alone. Drank her coffee alone. This wasn't what she had signed up for. Not at all. Over the last few months, everything had gone to hell, and she was tired of not having control of her own destiny. From the minute that gang of scummy miscreants took her, she hadn't had control of anything. And it was time she changed that.

She stared at the burner phone. Okay. So, she'd promised Grier she wouldn't call, she would wait for him to make sure it was secure. And she'd sworn to him she wouldn't hop on the next plane out and show up at the clubhouse. But she hadn't said a damned thing about shooting a text to Hamilton, her friend, who she missed. Nothing wrong with talking to a friend she missed.

She picked up the phone, tapped his number into the keypad, then took the next ten minutes trying to remember how to send a text on a phone that flipped open and closed. Grier would be pissed if he found out she was communicating with Hamilton. Phones could be tracked. Even burner phones. But she couldn't just sit here on her hands. If he knew her at all, he would understand. Still, her stomach rolled.

She typed in the message, then looked at it for a minute before she slapped the phone closed and threw it on the bed. "Shit."

The baby cooed next to her, and Fiona closed her eyes, trying to imagine how things back home would go. And no matter how hard she tried, she couldn't get past the fact that Tyler Sedotal was ruthless. And determined. And cocky enough to be dangerous.

There was some comfort in knowing the guys trusted Grier now, but dammit, it should have been her back there with Hamilton and Jim and Sage. It should have been her forming the plan to take that bastard down. This was her club, her birthright, handed down to her by her father who'd built the damned thing into what it was. Yet, she was three-thousand miles away, holed up behind an iron gate, hiding like a coward.

Eli knocked on the open door and stood just outside the frame. She didn't move, as if she was waiting to be asked into a room in her own house. "You want to go to the market? They have… all kinds of…" She twitched her mouth to one side. "Stuff."

Their relationship hadn't progressed much past awkward and without Kye and Grier there to keep things going, no way could Fiona see how this would transform to anything more than stilted conversation and uncomfortable silences. But if Eli was willing to try, maybe Fiona could too. It would be nice to have someone to talk to about… everything. Since she didn't have Hamilton and Grier had gone home to take care of *her* business, this was her only choice.

She smiled at Eli, although it probably looked more like she was constipated, and nodded. "That sounds great." Who didn't like spending time with a former enemy? With someone she'd been taught to hate?

Still, she picked up the baby and walked out into the hallway. And shopped. Tasted. Sampled. Pretended she cared about the wares and products she'd purchased. Even made small talk, but Pine Hill was never further than a thought and a blink away.

The baby, neither impressed nor interested, fell asleep halfway through the market and stayed asleep until right around bedtime. This was the time that Grier would have taken over for a while, reading to her from motorcycle magazines or an old dog-eared western he'd apparently had for years, then giving her a bath and even singing to her before he handed her back for Fiona to feed.

This went on for the first few days and made Fiona

miss Grier even more. He hadn't called or sent a text. If not for Kye talking to Eliana the first night, Fiona wouldn't have known anything. Not about the influx of bikers in town. Not about the slowdown of street sales. All of which Grier should have told her himself. But he didn't. He didn't say a damned word about anything because he never called.

At three a.m. on the third day, she'd had enough. That was *her* husband, *her* club, and *her* fight. And by God, she was done hiding behind a gate letting Grier handle *her* business. The baby on the other hand…

London would have to stay with Eliana. That was all there was to it. Eli was like wonder mom. She could handle two babies. And Fiona could afford a nanny to help. What she couldn't help was the need to go back home and make those sons of bitches pay for putting her in hiding. It was time they learned the cold hard fact of life. Fiona Strong-Owen didn't hide. Not anymore.

By sun-up she was packed and ready. And she'd made a big pot of bribery coffee and a giant plate of persuasion pastries, cut some fruit and laid out a spread of eggs, bacon, and sausage.

Eliana walked into the kitchen and stared at the counter full of food. Without speaking, she poured a cup of coffee and sat at the table across from Fiona.

"I'm going home." No need for beating around the burning bush. If Eli put up a fight, there was always money, and she would pay dearly to ensure London's safety.

Eliana nodded. "I know." She frowned. "Are you sure you can't wait until next week?"

What would waiting until next week do to help the situation? Fiona shook her head. "I need to go now."

"Of course." Eli shrugged. "But just so you know, you are solely responsible for a very ugly French maid uniform I have to prance around in when Kye gets back." She sighed. "I bet you'd last at least two weeks. He said you wouldn't make it one."

They had an easy kind of relationship Fiona envied. Light-hearted. She and Grier hadn't managed to get there yet. They'd had moments, but their relationship had suffered so much from all the club stuff and the kidnapping and hiding out that drove them both crazy.

"I suppose London is staying here?"

And it was killing Fiona, but she couldn't take her baby into what would only be able to be described as a war zone. "Yeah, please."

"Damn!" Uh-oh. Eli's reply didn't bode well. "I told him there was no way you'd leave the baby with me. He said you wouldn't risk her safety no matter what the past said about us." She clicked her tongue.

Fiona cocked an eyebrow. "Sorry. But I can't take her back with me. It's too…" And there was no one else she could trust to care for London.

"Dangerous." Eli nodded. "I get it, you know. After what they did to you…" She pointed to her throat. "I would go back, too."

Eli had never been part of the biker world. Never liked anything about the club, and so Fiona's way of life probably didn't make a lot of sense. But she was grateful for Eli's support now. Grateful enough her eyes went misty again.

"Thanks." She hadn't had a lot of friends growing up. Too many big biker types hanging around scared the private school parents away from letting their daughters be friends with her, so Fiona spent most of her time with Hamilton and Grier. It was nice to have at least the hope of friendship now. But now, it was time to go. She had business to attend to back home.

* * *

THE MINUTE he stepped off the plane the FBI picked him up. More threats, more breathing down his neck and he didn't have time for it. And they'd kept him four days. Four extra days for Sedotal's tab. And because when the Demons discovered he'd been the one to kill Dave, the undercover FBI who'd posed as a driver for the Screaming Demons shipments of parts stuffed with drugs, they'd chopped Kale into pieces and sent him back to Sedotal a limb at a time, Grier couldn't even give the bastard up to the FBI. So, the FBI still wanted Hamilton and seemed rather hellbent on getting him, if the smackdown Grier had taken in an unmonitored interview room meant anything.

They'd given him a week to get them proof before they promised to come back with a SWAT team and a warrant for Grier's arrest for the same murder they were trying to pin on Hamilton. A week to find and kill Sedotal and figure out how to get them off his back.

He walked into the clubhouse. The empty clubhouse. He listened, heard only the sound of his own boots on the floor. Then he stopped. Not empty. Fiona's office door was open, and murmurs came from inside. He walked toward the door. Every remaining Demon in the city who wasn't out looking for Sedotal or tracking down leads stood circled around her desk.

He moved through the back row of guys, then pushed through the rest until he could see what they were all looking at. His mouth dropped open. "Fiona."

She smiled as if she wasn't supposed to be back in Belize, safe and sound at Kye's house with its gate and fences and privacy. "Hello, Grier. Good to see they let you go."

Goddammit. Someone had called her. Probably Hamilton. Her spy. "How'd you know?" Not that he could do much about it right now, not until she was back on a plane. But as soon as she was gone, there would be plenty of hell to pay.

"I came back and you weren't here. I called Sheriff Lodi and he told me." She walked out from behind the desk. "The new sheriff in town's on the payroll. Sage hacked into his computer and the information he found means we're going to own this guy for as long as he's sheriff." She grinned. "The boys have been busy while we were away."

"You could've just asked Kye."

Fiona's smile faded. "No one's seen him either."

What? As the FBI dragged him away, he'd seen Kye get into a taxi. Grier's gut ached. "Did your sheriff friend know anything?"

Fiona shook her head. "He hasn't been picked up."

That meant someone knew he was back. He'd lost the element of surprise and now the fuckers had Kye. Grier slammed his hand on Fiona's desk, and she looked at Sage. "I did a little computer stuff." No need to explain to Grier. He wouldn't get the techie terms, and Sage knew it, too. Probably why he didn't bother. "There are three buildings beside the dance studio listed in a dummy company's name. I figured if they owned the dance studio, chances are the Omens are using one of those. Hamilton put guys on all three. So far, we don't have any movement, but I'm still digging, and Hamilton has patrols going out, checking anything abandoned, out of the way, or remotely associated with Tyler Sedotal or Willy Carr." He glanced at the woman standing at the side of the room, chewing her thumbnail. "Mia gave us some other places they might be. We're watching them all."

That accounted for the low numbers at the clubhouse.

"And we are putting shipments out. If they're coming for us, they'll go after those first." Hamilton's voice was quiet, stern, and its usual gravel depth of baritone. Almost comforting in the light of finding out his wife had forsaken her own safety to come back and that Kye had been taken.

"I saw Kye get into a cab at the airport." They'd dressed like tourists to try to escape notice. "He was wearing a Bruins jersey and jeans, I think."

"It'll take a while to talk to every driver that covers the airport." The girl in the corner spoke quietly. She stood and walked to stand beside Sage.

"When did you guys figure out he was missing?" The longer the Omens had gone without calling for ransom, the worse it would be for Kye. Could even be revenge for Kale. Fuck. He'd have to tell Eli.

"This morning when I got here. I asked about him." Fiona nodded. "But I know that he's talked to Eli since you guys got here. So… maybe he's out on his own? Looking?" From her face, she didn't buy it either.

It wasn't like he could call Eli and ask when the last time she spoke to him was. Not without tipping her off and having to worry about her safety too, because if Kye was in danger and she knew it, no man in the world would be big enough to stop her from coming back here. "We have to find him." He glanced at Fiona. "What did he say when he talked to Eli?"

She shifted and crossed her arms. "He mentioned extra bikers in town and a slowdown of street sales."

Grier nodded. That meant Kye had been out talking to the gangs and the little preppie college boys who handled the merchandise at the street level. "When did he call?"

"A while after your flight landed, I think. She never mentioned if he called again."

Fuck. This was not a wrinkle he wanted to deal with. And if Kye was out there somewhere playing the hero on his own, friendship or not, Grier was going to kill him. And if anything happened to Kye…

Fiona leaned in to talk to Sage, then stood at her full height, a height enhanced more with the heels she must have changed into from the flip flops she'd loved on the beach. She had a slow, confident smile when she looked out at the men in the room. "All right. This is what we're going to do."

15

They had confirmation from one of their street dealers; the Omens had picked up Kye. Took him in broad daylight on the corner of Hampshire and Cambridge. She'd had Sage try to track his phone, but the damned thing was turned off. But Fiona knew in her gut that where they found Kye, they would find Sedotal.

Grier paced in front of her desk like he was stuck in some kind of cage. Six steps forward, military turn, six steps back. And repeat. She watched him. His body was a coil, ready to spring into action.

"What do you think you're doing, Fiona? What the fuck do you think you're doing?"

Oh, the anger. "I'm doing what I was meant to do, Grier. I'm handling this business, this... shit." Well, she could summon anger, too. "You need to calm down. We're going to find Kye."

"Before his arm comes back in a box? Or his leg? Maybe an eyeball? Before they brand him, too?" And more pacing.

She moved around her desk to stand in his path. "Stop." Although she had no answer. Killing Kye would draw Grier out. That had to be why they'd taken him. And as much as she hated to admit it, there was only one way to get Kye back.

"I have to give them me." And he'd just said it.

She stared. Any other of the men, she would have agreed without any hesitation, but this was Grier. Her husband. The man she would have died for. And he felt that same devotion to Kye.

"Okay." The Omens had muscle and God knew what else, but Fiona had Sage, and he had gadgets and technology. "Come on." She led him out into the bar area and sat across the table from Sage. "We're sending Grier in to get Kye back. Put word out. Something that lets them know where he's going to be. Somewhere open where we can control the traffic and the view." He'd been a leader with Hamilton while she'd been hiding her head in fear and shame, licking her wounds while he and Hamilton took care of everything.

Fiona's stomach churned, but damned if she could show weakness right now. She needed to keep her shit together, be the woman her father taught her to be. Falling apart would have to wait.

"All right. Where are we thinking?"

Privacy would be a must. A place where they could see everything coming in and out. "Tell them we'll be at the old compound."

"We burned it… after Jez."

Not the greatest of news. "Okay. But there's only one way in, and we can control everything about it. The road, the tunnels, every tree and branch is ours if we get in there and set it up, get Sedotal somewhere I'm the one in charge." And it was about damned time, too. Even if it sounded grandiose and narcissistic, and she wasn't one to believe in destiny or higher powers, but this was what she was meant to do. What Max planned. And now it was time to live up to it.

"Fiona, you can't be there." Grier yanked the chair next to her and twisted it so he could straddle it. "It's too dangerous."

"Oh, please." She waved a hand. "I'm the one with the brands. I know the danger. And I am going to be the one who kills him. You can each have a shot at him, take a piece for yourselves, but his life is mine." She needed vengeance. Retribution. To watch the life drain out of his eyes and onto the pavement or dirt or concrete. Fiona would exact her revenge.

"I'm the one he wants."

She nodded. "And that's why you're the bait."

"Do you think he won't expect this? You think he'll just agree to walk into what any dumbass is going to know is a trap?"

Men and their egos were as predictable as the heat in the summer and cold in the winter. "To get you, yeah. You're Tyler's kryptonite." In a very different way than he was hers. "He'll come because he won't be able to stay away, especially if he thinks it's a trap. He'll want to show that he doesn't fear you and that he doesn't consider you a threat." Predictable.

Sage nodded. Grier scowled. Fiona continued. "But he won't be walking into your trap. He's walking into mine. And that's how we're going to get him."

She was thinking old fashioned nets in trees, trip-wires, underground explosives. But Sage took a long swallow of his beer then slammed the bottle onto the table. "Did you notice the bikes they ride?" Fiona hadn't. Grier shrugged and gave off a make and model. "Right. Pricey. New. Bells and whistles out the tailpipe." He grinned. "Onboard computer technology." When Fiona widened her eyes, he shrugged and clucked his tongue against his teeth. "I did some reading."

He laid out a plan that sounded like something right out of some futuristic sci-fi flick. But if he could make it happen, no member of the Omens would make it past the drive in.

"And you can do that?"

He laughed like she'd asked if he knew how to tie his shoes. "You bet."

This was all coming together. "All right. Then let's get to work. How long do you need?"

"A couple of hours." He pulled a laptop from under the table and the clicking and clacking of keys began. It might not have been musical, but to Fiona, it was a symphony.

It took a while to get everything organized and planned, but Hamilton left to put out the word and get the guys back. They were all meeting at the compound, and it was almost time.

When they were all assembled at the compound, Fiona sat alone with Grier in one of the shells of a cabin that hadn't burned completely to the ground. "You're mad."

He hadn't so much as looked at her since she and Sage sat planning at the table. He grunted a response that could have been a yes or a denial that doubled as a lie.

"I don't know how much time we have, but if you want to fight it out… I'm right here."

"You should be in Belize with Eli."

She chuckled as if any of this was funny, as if any of the things they'd been through weren't hanging over their heads and wouldn't continue hanging over their head until this was over. "Well, I felt like I belonged here, taking care of the club and taking care of you."

He shook his head. "The club. That's what this is about?"

She hadn't seen him angry often and the intensity of it surprised her almost as much as how he could twist her words into something she didn't mean. "No, Einstein. It's about you and us and me. *I* need to be here to see this through so *we* can get on with our lives and *you* can stop blaming yourself. But it's also about the club and what it meant to my dad and how I won't let it go to some cheap shot loser who thinks he can be Max."

"And you think you can be Max?" His disbelief struck something in her, a deeper, darker anger than any she'd felt before. She might have expected it from Kye or Sage or even Hamilton, but not from Grier.

"I know I can." Ruthlessness was part of the nurture versus nature debate, and that same ruthlessness had cycled through her childhood. "So, just stay out of my way, Grier."

The first shot ricocheted off a tree, missing everything but leafy branches, but the unmistakable ping said the time had come. It had started.

Grier listened. More shots. More bikes. The screech of brakes locking up. The thwack of bodies falling. He glanced at Fiona. His warrior princess. Rifle in hand, pistol in her waistband.

They'd planned for Sage and Hamilton to take four Omens to "interrogate," who would either lead them to Kye or die. Sedotal wasn't to be touched. Not by anyone but Fiona or Grier.

From his spot, Grier watched Hamilton dragging one of the motorcycle riders behind a tree. They hadn't counted on the Omens bringing Kye along, in a van that slipped past Kye's computer trap. The black, windowless vehicle sped to the center of the compound and slid to a dusty stop. The side panel door opened, and Tyler Sedotal stepped out with a gun in one hand and Kye in the other.

"Come out, come out wherever you are." Sedotal sing-songed the words then deadpanned, "Or I'll blow his fucking head off right now."

Grier caught Fiona by the arm. If he'd let her, she would've walked out there and shot first. Not that he could blame her, but she was their element of surprise. Their only one now, since Sedotal coming in this way had voided the others. "Stay here. He won't expect you to be here." He walked toward the door. "If you get a good shot, take it." When she nodded, he added, "Don't come out until you've taken him down, Fiona." Fury darkened her eyes. "I mean it." Softer he added, "I love you."

She nodded to the opening. "Go."

They'd underestimated Sedotal. They'd not given him enough credit, and now, he had Kye as his human shield. Grier raised the shotgun Sedotal would eventually force him to put down and walked out. Since this wasn't Kye's first hostage situation—he'd once been Max's right hand, a hot commodity for other clubs as a bargaining chip—he walked ahead, not struggling, but not making it easy for Sedotal to move him either. His steps stuttered and Sedotal yanked him backward, closer to his body. And since Kye towered over him, the amount of space Fiona had to take her shot shrunk.

"Had your wife, now I've got your boyfriend. Hard couple of weeks, huh?" Sedotal smirked at Grier and took a hold of Kye's hair, jerking his head back. "Did your wife tell you the fun we had?"

"She said you weren't man enough to get it up." She hadn't said anything much at all about her time with him. "Is that because your dick doesn't work, or do you prefer your dates more masculine?"

"My dick's fine. Ask your wife." Grier ignored the jibes and stared hard at Sedotal. Gun hand extended toward Grier shaking. Twitchy left eye. Nerves. Maybe nerve damage. Either way, an advantage.

"Already did. I think she said small and broken.

Doesn't matter. You're dealing with me now and I don't give a shit about your dick."

"I would rather deal with her. Where is she?"

And like they didn't have a plan, like she didn't give a good god damn about her own safety she walked out of the cabin. "I'm right here." Her grin, if something so evil could be called that, was darker than anything Grier had ever seen. His heart faltered. "And I gotta say all this witty banter is thrilling, but not really why we're here. So, are you done stalling?"

Sedotal stared at Fiona. "You're awfully brave for someone wearing my brand next to her pussy." She didn't talk, just kept grinning that sick little smile. "Put your gun down or your boy dies."

Fiona scoffed. "Not my boy. He's a traitor. Shoot him if you want." Grier couldn't tell if she meant it or not. She spoke with a quiet ferocity. "He was never one of us anyway."

Kye, whose face resembled a sad, misshapen clown's whose makeup had run in all the worst ways, lifted his head to stare at Fiona. "Bitch."

Grier's gut clenched at the slide of metal on metal and the unmistakable click of the bolt. She'd loaded a shell into the chamber. And this time, Grier wasn't sure who she planned to shoot. "Move him. I'll get rid of him and you can deal with me. Just the way you wanted." She ground the words out as he shoved Kye to the ground.

Fiona shifted the rifle and aimed at Kye. Sedotal aimed at Fiona, Grier aimed at him. Kye remained on the ground with a rifle pointed at him. He lifted his head, looked at Fiona, winked, and reached as if asking for help. She tossed him the rifle, he twisted around and aimed at Sedotal as Fiona pulled the pistol from behind her back. Now three guns aimed at Sedotal.

The evil in her smile deepened. "You seem to have a choice. You can shoot one of us and the other two will open fire and you're gonna be nothing but a bad memory. Or you can put your shit down now and do as you're told."

Grier waited as Tyler threw his head back and laughed. "You always let your bitch talk for you?"

He shrugged. "I like the sound of her voice."

Tyler aimed at Fiona but stared at Grier. "I like when she cries in pain." Why hadn't Fiona fired? This could all be over. "Do you know what a duel is?"

"A duel?"

He wobbled his head from side to side. "In the old days, when two men had a dispute, they settled it with a gunfight. Ten paces, spin, and draw."

Stupidest thing Grier had ever heard. Besides, he could drop the fucker right now if he hadn't promised Fiona he would wait. No need for some hoity-toity duel. "Nah. I'm good."

"Chicken shit."

Grier shrugged and Sedotal fired at Fiona. She went down, he turned. And Kye fired. But Hamilton had already clotheslined Sedotal.

Blood seeped from a wound at the side of Fiona's head. Grier's heart stopped. This couldn't be happening. She was supposed to be safe, in Belize with their baby. And again, Grier had failed her.

16

Seven stitches. Angry, check that, furious husband. And in the commotion, Sedotal managed to get away.

Grier drove her home. In silence. He didn't speak at all right up to the minute he walked behind her into the house and slammed the door shut behind him. "What the hell were you thinking?"

She didn't answer. What could she say that wouldn't make this worse? A half-inch, maybe less, to the left and Fiona would be dead. As it was, the bullet grazed her just over her ear leaving her with a bald patch and a splitting headache. And the aforementioned angry husband.

"I was thinking..." She'd been tired of hiding. That was what she was thinking.

"He could have killed you."

"Could have killed you, too." Not to point out the obvious but, "Yet, here we both are."

"I left you in Belize because…" He raked his hand through his hair. "Because I couldn't stand the thought of losing you." He turned away from her then back again. "But the whole world revolves around what you want, huh?"

"What does that mean?"

He opened his mouth then snapped it shut. "He could've shot you, Fiona."

"He did." Her mouth leaped without looking.

"Exactly!" He stalked out to the kitchen, opened the refrigerator then slammed it shut. "I gotta get some air."

And by air, he meant a drink. Probably something black labeled that would burn all the way to his belly, but would also make him forget he was mad at her. "Go."

She didn't feel like fighting anyway. Her head was killing her, and she just wanted to sleep.

"I'm not leaving you here alone."

She didn't need a sitter. "Just go. I'm fine." Instead of standing around to continue the argument, she climbed the steps and went to her room. Never had a bed looked so inviting, or sheets felt so cool against her skin.

A moment later the door shut, and Grier crawled in next to her, pulled her back against his chest and breathed in deep, burying his head in her hair. "Please go back to Belize, Fiona. I can't do everything I have to do and worry about you, too."

She sighed. This was her fight as much as his. The baby was safe with Eliana and she had to see this through. "I'm not going back to Belize." And she'd come up to bed so she didn't have to argue, not so he could follow her and continue the discussion that would most definitely lead to an argument. But since there was nothing she liked more than Grier holding her, she didn't get up and head down to the sofa.

"Fine." His tone, the tension in his body, said it wasn't fine at all, but she remained silent. Some things he had to work out for himself. Her independence, it turned out, was one of them. "How's your head?"

"It's okay." Not entirely true. It ached. But nothing so substantial she wouldn't be able to sleep through it. The nagging in her brain, though, the idea that someone had let Tyler go, bothered her enough it would be a very long time before she managed to close her eyes and quiet her brain. "Grier, how did Sedotal get away?" She turned toward him.

"I don't know. You went down, and I didn't see anything else." But Grier wasn't a good enough liar for her to believe that.

"Hmm." But it would have to wait until the morning to figure it out, when her head wasn't throbbing. "How's Kye?" Last she'd seen, he looked like the live-action version of a punching bag. And she knew the feeling.

"He's gonna be fine. His face was too pretty, anyway. This'll add some character." His voice went light, but she heard the relief. "Did you have that whole thing worked out with him where you threw him the rifle?"

Oh, that she had that much foresight. "No. It was spur of the moment. Could have turned out bad if he hadn't caught it, I guess." And that was as close to regret as she could give him.

Grier's arms tightened around her. "Yeah."

BY MORNING, she was no closer to figuring out how Sedotal got free than she'd been when she first went to bed. And it wasn't because she hadn't laid there thinking. She'd seen Hamilton creep up behind him and grab him. But after that, everything blurred into everything else. Next thing she remembered she was riding in an ambulance. And they'd lost him.

She slipped out of bed and went downstairs for coffee, stopping on her way through the living room to fluff a throw pillow. As she walked into the kitchen, she stopped. "How the hell did you get in here?"

"Twenty-dollar door lock, twenty-four-year-old shoulder." Sedotal pointed his gun at the chair across from him. "I was going to wake you up, but you and big brother looked too cozy. Sit down."

She sat. There were a hundred things she wanted to know, but her mouth wouldn't move, wouldn't let her form a question. Who had helped him escape, why he was so fascinated with Grier, and so many more questions she couldn't even sort them. Instead, she waited for him to speak.

"I spent a lot of time thinking about you last night and you know what I came up with?" Not that she cared, but she tilted her head, studying him. He looked perfectly healthy, short blonde hair spikey and freshly gelled, clean, expensive clothes. Not a bruise on him. Hardly fair when her head felt like she'd stumbled and landed forehead first on a rusty railroad spike. "I think you must be part cat. And the way I figure it, you have seven lives left."

"I could say the same about you."

He lifted the gun and aimed at her face. "I'm going to take care of it right now." She saw the muzzle flash and opened her mouth to scream.

"Hey, Fiona, wake up." Grier leaned over her, one arm under her neck, the hand of his free arm cradling her cheek. "Come on, baby. It was just a dream."

A dream. Yeah. That made sense since she wasn't sitting there with face splattered all over her kitchen cabinets. She related the details. "Maybe it's your brain trying to tell you we need to replace the door locks."

Maybe, but Fiona knew it was more. It was her subconscious telling her she wasn't fit to run this club, couldn't handle the pressure, had gone soft. Shit.

* * *

FIONA WAS HAVING NIGHTMARES. Grier couldn't figure out how Sedotal managed to get away, how to keep his wife safe, how he would break her the news that could shatter her, or how to put an end to all of this. But he had Fiona in his arms and there was nothing he wanted more than to stay right there in their bed, in their house, snuggled together, pretending nothing bad could touch them. But his text messages said that wasn't to be. Sage was on his way.

Good news in one respect, if Sage had information that would lead them to Sedotal. Bad news if Sage had information that would lead them to Sedotal. Besides, He had a few good reasons to stay in bed—Fiona wrapped around him, the thunderstorm brewing outside, the fact that he had no idea how to keep his wife safe—but he had as many to get up. They needed to figure out their next move. Hopefully, Sage had a good idea; ex-military guys always had ideas.

He disentangled Fiona's arms and walked to the

bathroom. Occasionally, when he was belting out the hits in the shower, an idea struck him, something powerful, something that would make a difference. And God, he needed one of those today.

But nothing came. His mind was too clouded. Not in the shower. Or over his first cup of coffee or as he sat at the table with Sage. Of all the things bothering him, staring at Sage, only one mattered. Grier had seen Mia push Hamilton, and that had ended worse than he could have predicted. And it gave Sedotal just enough time to disappear into the woods.

He watched Sage fiddle with his mug of coffee. But this had to be said. Although, word around the club was that Sage had a real soft spot for this girl, more than any other woman in the place. "Fiona's going to kill her you know." He was talking about Mia. The woman who would take all the blame. "You trust her?"

Sage lifted his head. "I do."

"So, you think her loyalty is to us now? They branded her. She's one of them."

"They branded Fiona, too. Twice." Everyone knew about the one on Fiona's neck. But the one on her leg was top secret. "Are you doubting Fiona?"

Grier shifted in his chair, thought about everything he knew. "Why did Mia push Ham?"

A long pause stretched between them, then a sigh. "She said Fiona deserved to kill him, not you, not Ham."

Convenient story. One with an ending he wouldn't have been able to predict if ever he tried. "So, she let him go? What if he gets Fiona first? Did she think about that?" His gut flared with anger. There was no way that flimsy story would fly. "We could've ended this yesterday. Now, who knows what's going to happen." Fiona was the unpredictable variable in the new scenario. "She did this, Sage. I don't see Fiona forgiving this one."

"Look, I'm gonna tell you everything I know. She came in for them, tried to use me. It was… I was gullible. But she was too perfect, you know, too pleasing. I called her on it. She said…" He broke off. Apparently, what she'd said was private and it could stay that way until Grier found out it affected the club. "Anyway, we can trust her now. You have my word." He shook his head. "I know it looks bad, what she did to Ham, but she didn't do it to let Tyler go free. She did it for Fiona."

He didn't trust Mia, but he trusted Sage. Even though he could see holes in that story big enough to drive a truck through. But he nodded. "Just to be on the safe side, Mia stays back from here on out. If I were you, I'd hide her until we see how Fiona is. I know you trust her, but this is my wife and my family."

"Yeah." Sage nodded. "Did you tell Fiona about Ham yet?"

He should have, but she'd been shot, and he couldn't do it. And he was being punished for it. Every time he closed his eyes, he saw Mia hit Hamilton from the side, saw Sedotal wheel around, poised to shoot Fiona or Grier, but the bullet… the way his arm shot out as the gun fired, the trajectory and the happenstance of Hamilton falling to Sedotal's right… Grier's eyes snapped open.

"No."

"What about Ham?" Fiona stood in the doorway, hair mussed, eyes heavy with fatigue, skin with its early morning glow. Grier stood, turned to her, and with every second that ticked off the clock, he could see the awareness change her face, the droop to her mouth, the tears in her eyes, the lines deepening on her face. "Grier, what about Ham?" He couldn't answer more than a slight shake to his head, and she moved in until her chest aligned with his and her fist beat against him, pounding her sadness into him.

"I'm so sorry, Fi."

Her breath hitched and she sobbed, still punching but with less force, less anger and more grief. "No!" Her screams tore at him, broke something that connected all his pieces. He would have sold his soul to keep her from this pain. He would have died if it would have helped.

"Listen, we can leave now. Say fuck it all and go back to our baby and Belize. We don't have to be here." He just wanted to ease the pain for her, and he didn't know how.

She shoved him back, fury and rage as powerful as his in her eyes. "Leave?" She scoffed and swiped her tears away. "He was my best friend. My. Best. Friend." Grier nodded because she wasn't finished. "You have one day to find that son of a bitch and bring him to me."

"Fiona…"

"Bring. Him. To. Me." She turned and walked out of the kitchen.

She hadn't asked for much since they got married, but now that she had, there was no way Grier would let her down.

17

There was no funeral for Hamilton, no urn to cherish, no casket to bury. The FBI turned his body over to his family back in Chicago, a family he'd hated and run away from, a family who didn't appreciate the beauty of this man.

Fiona stood at the front of the room, whiskey glass in hand, and looked out at the men standing and sitting who'd come to pay respects to Hamilton. The grief had given way to fury, but she owed Hamilton this tribute, these words.

"Damian Hamilton was one of the best of us. He took his oath when he was sixteen, and from that day forward he was Screaming Demon, inside and out. No brother he wouldn't have died to defend, no risk he wouldn't have taken for the club." She swallowed back the lump in her throat, blinked away the tears. "Max always said there was something about Ham that made him special. His loyalty. His compassion. The badass that came shining through when we needed him. I say there was not *something* special about Damian Hamilton. *Everything* about him was special." She lifted her glass and a tear slipped down her cheek. There was so much more to say. Hell, she'd recite the dictionary if it meant she didn't have to say her final goodbye. Hamilton. Her friend was gone, and the reality made her guts hurt.

The woman was gone. She'd left sometime in the night. Coward. Traitor. Bitch. Those were the words Fiona had ascribed to Mia Giovanni. She'd put out another order early, after she'd finally convinced Grier to tell her what had happened. Not only were they to find Sedotal, but she'd also charged Sage with bringing Mia back. Whether he did it or not would determine if she let him live. There was no way Hamilton's death would go unanswered. And Fiona didn't give a damn who answered for it.

Because she couldn't bring herself to say goodbye, she closed her eyes, pictured Hamilton and drank her cup dry. She walked out of the bar, out of the clubhouse, her .38 hidden under her shirt, a .22 strapped to her thigh under her dress, and a .45 in her purse. Someone was going to die today.

She drove home, thinking. Always thinking. Hamilton was gone. Grier was out with Sage searching, and the guys all had their orders. But Fiona had nothing to do but wait, to decide who she let live and who would die.

She drove to the house, changed into a pair of jeans and a t-shirt, tied her hair back and opened the garage. Her bike sat ignored in the corner under a drop cloth. But today, she wanted to ride. She wanted to drive away from her thoughts, to outrun her anger.

She rode until the wind burned her skin until she had to stop for a drink. She pulled into a service station and parked the bike in front of the attached restaurant.

The place smelled like fried food and burgers and its red leather booths and black and white checkered floors were pulled from an era gone by. More importantly, the place was full, and she slipped in unnoticed among the clinking of silverware, the murmurs of conversation, and the bustling waitresses. Just what she needed.

She took a seat at the counter and ordered a soda. Her cell buzzed in her pocket, but she ignored it. She wanted food and to be left alone. She didn't turn to look at the man next to her or the family in the booth at the corner. Didn't care about the couple arguing at the table or the woman yanking her toddler behind her to the bathroom. She cared that Hamilton had died, and her heart hurt.

The morning had slipped by her and now the after-noon wasted away as she sat at least two hundred miles from home. And it wasn't like she didn't have choices. She could just ride away. The need for revenge would fade. She could go back to Belize, be there in a couple of days… hold London. Disappearing from there wouldn't be hard. Or she could go back and see this through, take care of business, avenge Hamilton and make them all pay. Shamefully, as a mother she wanted her baby, but the call for retribution was too strong. She needed it.

Her stomach and heart ached with equal intensity, and she stood. Time to head back, to her real life.

As she started her bike, she took a glance down the road. Two hundred miles from home. What the hell was a Screaming Demons truck doing here? And she knew it was one of theirs from the horned skeleton emblem on the mud flaps. Max had created the design himself. Instead of turning toward home, she pulled out behind the truck.

Another hundred miles and two left turns later, the truck turned into a warehouse lot. Fiona watched from the curb. Two guys, neither old enough to drink and probably not to even drive, came around the back and lifted the door. The taller, stockier of the two climbed inside and disappeared into the darkness. A minute later, he reappeared with Mia, bound by zip ties, eyes hidden behind a blindfold that looked suspiciously like a sleep mask, and gagged with a bandana that had seen better days. The guy on the ground lifted her down and they took turns pushing her toward the warehouse.

Fiona watched them push a code into a keypad then go inside. "Well, I'll be damned." If she believed in signs or the afterlife, she might've believed Hamilton had led her here, but she didn't. Mostly. Instead, she snuck inside the gate on foot. Hid behind the truck and pulled her .38.

She hadn't stumbled into the middle of a mystery. She'd uncovered the Omen hideout. One of them anyway. And a Screaming Demon truck. And she had an idea.

She slid around to the driver side. Her plan would either work, or she'd die. Today, she didn't particularly care which.

* * *

GRIER PULLED up beside Fiona's bike. Sage had started tracking her phone as soon as Jim called and said she'd walked out of the service for Hamilton. And Grier had stayed back, letting her have this time alone, but keeping her always in sight.

Right now, he just couldn't believe his eyes. She'd run the stolen truck through the front of the warehouse. Straight through. Then, like some kind of modern-day

Annie Oakley, she'd burst from the cab, gun in hand, and started firing.

Grier ran in behind her. He didn't call out to her but threw down some cover fire of his own as she rolled behind a crate. He flanked her on the left as she peeled around the box. "What are you doing here?"

"Following you." He listened for movement, for the reloads, for more than the groan of the guy caught between the truck and a wall.

Fiona slid to the right behind another crate. "They have Mia."

Grier looked over the top of his hiding spot then dropped down when a shot whizzed past his ear. Fuck. They could certainly use a few extra Demons. "We should fall back." When she lifted her brows at him, he fired wildly over the top of the crate without standing. "It means—"

"I know what it means." She snapped the words at him. "We can't leave her here."

No, they couldn't. But they also couldn't stay where they were while the place filled up with more guns, locked and loaded, aiming at them. Fiona glared at Grier as he motioned her toward the opening the truck had ripped through the wall.

"I'm not leaving her."

Which meant Grier wasn't leaving either. It also meant they needed to get somewhere safer, somewhere they could regroup. He checked the clip in his gun. Shit. They needed to regroup somewhere with shells for a couple of .38s.

Thank God for technology. He ripped off a text to Sage then covered his head with his arms and moved toward Fiona. He followed her to the other side of the truck and around toward the front.

Nothing good was going to come of this, but he stayed close to her. He would die to protect her, but as he tried to move in front of her, she switched direction, veered away, as if her anger wasn't singularly for the people who'd taken Mia. Not that he could blame her. She'd had some rough days of late.

They hadn't been shot at for a few seconds and Fiona's step grew more confident. But they were hundreds of miles from help. Fiona stepped out into the open and looked around as if they hadn't just taken heavy fire. With her gun at her side, she moved as if she didn't give a damn what happened to her. She could have as easily been window shopping at the mall for all the consideration she gave for her safety. Hamilton dying had broken something inside her.

They moved further into the room and she kicked one of the bodies. He couldn't have been more than twenty, and probably not that old. Just a kid following the orders of a guy who was his idol. Fuck. He'd been that kid once.

"This is the driver of the truck." She nodded to the other body. Another kid. His acne hadn't even cleared up. "That's his buddy." With a growl, she drew her foot back and slammed it into his head. Once. Twice. Again. She'd earned this rage, this fury.

Grier looked up. High ceiling. No catwalks. No dangling chains. This looked like nothing more than a storage facility. The floors were concrete and dirty, windows high on the walls were jagged with broken glass. Debris in corners. Paint peeling. A heavy metal door leading further into the building. And of course, Fiona bee-lined for it. Grier's gut churned. Whatever waited behind that door wouldn't be sunshine and flowers. Still, she turned the knob. The metal ground against the floor as she tugged it open.

The smell in this place had to be toxic, a mixture of chemicals, exhaust fumes, and sweat. She walked ahead of him onto a carpeted floor, an office portion of the building, her back pressed against the wall, although there was nothing to provide cover if anyone burst out from whatever hiding space they'd chosen. The space between them widened as she hurried now, and Grier widened his steps to catch her. She had no fear, opening doors and poking her head inside. Each time, Grier's heart stopped until she pulled it closed and moved to the next.

They made it to the end of the hallway and another

door. She put her hand on the knob and looked back at Grier. She didn't need his permission, probably would have gone in without it, but he gave her a nod. She pushed it open. More metal scratching on concrete, this time a hail of gunfire came with it. She kept her back against the wall and called out. "Mia, if you can hear me, it's Fiona. I'm going to save you."

Grier waited. More shots. At least two shooters by the number. They knew nothing about the room, could only guess the number of people in there, would be sitting ducks with the small amount of firepower between them. But when he grabbed her elbow, she shook him off and walked in. She shot twice as Grier rounded the corner behind her. Now they had to find Mia.

18

Fiona stared at Sage and Mia, the way he touched her, and looked at her, the way he cared. He could try to hide behind a blankness in his face, but his eyes said everything. She'd felt that way about Grier. Probably still did once she got past all the other stuff, the grief, the anger, even the disbelief.

Grier stood beside her. She could hear his still unsettled breathing, feel his body shaking as he took her hand. He, too, watched Sage with Mia. "You need to get her somewhere safe. They aren't going to stop coming for her."

Sage nodded to Fiona. "Or her."

Grier gave her hand a squeeze, and she wanted to pull away because even that slight touch made her want to lean on his strength.

Instead, she lifted her head. "I can handle myself."

Although, she hadn't managed to think of the second and third gun in her backpack before she climbed in and drove the truck through the warehouse. That could have been a costly mistake. Especially if there had been more than four Omens in the warehouse, but since there had been just the four, everything had turned out fine.

"You going to sleep with your guns on you?" Fiona shrugged at Sage's flip question, and Sage glanced at Grier. "Then you, my friend, should sleep with your eyes open."

"Yeah. I got that feeling, too." He shielded his anger behind a smile, but Fiona could still feel it.

Mia leaned into Sage and winced with each step as he helped her out of the clubhouse. And Grier waited until they were alone before he dropped Fiona's hand and spun to stare at her. "We need to talk."

No, they didn't. They needed to find a way to put an end to this. "Talking" could wait.

She turned and walked toward her office. Of course he followed, stomping in and slamming the door shut behind him. He thought she wanted privacy, but she wanted silence. Not that he had the power to give it to her. Not unless he could crawl into her mind and find a way to duct tape her thoughts into submission.

She wheeled to face him. Maybe if they got this part of the day over with, they could move on and get to work on the important stuff.

He clamped his mouth shut, and since he was the one who "needed" this chat, she waited. Finally, he sighed. "You want to tell me what that was all about?"

"They had Mia."

"The woman you wanted to kill a few hours earlier."

Valid point. But he hadn't accounted for the fact that Fiona knew firsthand what Mia would suffer in that warehouse. "She wasn't there by choice."

"Still doesn't mean you should go off half-cocked and drive a truck through the building. It was stupid, and they could've killed you, Fiona." His green eyes flashed to a smoky emerald and he grabbed her by the shoulders.

Fiona couldn't help the flinch at his touch, and he dropped his hands, let go, and took a step back. Hurt replaced his anger, and she cleared her throat. She didn't mean to cringe, hated that it happened, but if she let go of the anger now, she would break, probably shatter to a thousand pieces. And an apology would push the shame forward and the anger out.

"Well, my stupidity saved her life, because they sure as hell didn't bring her there to tickle her with feathers." The venom in her voice made it deeper, more powerful. Just what she needed to stay in control. "And I didn't have anyone I could count on. I wanted her to know she did." Her arrow hit the mark, and his mouth twitched.

"You think I didn't care?" He spoke quietly, controlled, but there was an unmistakable disbelief.

She needed this fight, needed to build her anger until nothing he said or did would break it down. "Well, I was the one getting my ass beat every day. Didn't see you anywhere around. I mean, you were here, right? Telling one of the Kats to get on her knees? Or bending one over the bar so you could—"

"Stop it!" He stalked closer, and she held every bit of her ground. Her pulse kicked up, not from fear, but from excitement. From need. "I would never fuck around on you, and you know it." His breaths came in short labored puffs, and she closed the distance between them, crushed his mouth with hers. There was more than one way to work out her aggression.

Grier kissed her back, tried to slow it down, held onto her hand when she went for his shirt, but she wriggled free and yanked it up.

"Fiona."

She pulled away, hating herself for the doubt that sneaked around her anger to come to the front. "Too damaged?"

He took her face between his hands. "Too angry." Then he kissed her so soft, so slow, caressing her lips with his, inviting, enticing, so perfectly wrong for what she needed, and tears welled.

She ran her hands down his chest, over the lines of

muscles in his stomach, to his belt. Again, he stopped her.

"Dammit, Grier. I want this."

He grinned. "Me, too." His fingers tangled in her hair, and he leaned his forehead against hers. "But today, I want to worship you."

"I don't want to be worshiped." She wanted him to take control, to tell her what to do, to fuck her until her thoughts stopped rolling through her head.

"Oh yeah, you do." He slipped his fingers under the tiny strap of her tank top and slid them down her arm. "We'll do hard and fast, we'll do sexy and hot, but first, we're going to go slow, and I'm going to kiss every inch of your body, touch you in ways that make you hot and wet and sigh and moan. I'm going to make sure you know that your body is yours, but your soul is mine." He ran his lips from her jaw to her collarbone, licking, sucking, nibbling. Every swipe of his tongue went straight to her core. Every soft murmur against her skin went to her heart. But she wanted more, needed the skin to skin contact, to lose herself in the frenzy. But when she sped up, he held her back. When she pressed forward, he pulled an imaginary brake until she surrendered the control of the moment.

He walked them toward the sofa, his mouth melded to hers, then laid her down. And just when she thought he meant to take the next step, to "worship" her, he wrapped his arms around her shoulders and tucked her into his chest.

"Grier, please." Maybe if she asked nicely, which she knew he liked, he would give in and let her have what she wanted. God, she hoped so, because her cells were about to explode with need.

"Shh." He stroked her arm. "You're so strong, I know that. And I love you so much, love being with you, love making love with you." He kissed the top of her head. "I don't know what you need, or how to make you hurt less."

She stared up at him, saw the desire in his eyes, felt it in the way he held his body against hers, and loved the way he wanted her. "Make me forget. Even if it's just for a few minutes or hours. I don't want to think about anything but you."

For a second he didn't speak. A slow smile curved his lips. "All right."

It couldn't fix what was wrong, but if she could just have one moment of peace, she could find her next later.

He kissed her, another agonizing touch, slow and gentle. She pushed her tongue into his mouth, ran her hands under his shirt, ground her hips against his.

Oh, God. She needed him. When he deepened the kiss and pulled her leg over his hip to push against her, she moaned and used her calf muscles to urge him closer.

Her heart pulsed with need. She sat up and pushed his shirt over his head then tossed her shirt onto the pile with his. "Fiona…" His head dipped to take one already pebbled nipple into his mouth. His tongue swirled, and she held his head, let him move to the other side.

Grier flipped her onto her back and held himself over her, lowering his hips to rub his cock against her. "Please." She could only beg.

He kissed her again, no longer soft and gentle. Thank God. His tongue thrust into her mouth, dueled with hers. When he pulled away, he stood and shoved his jeans down. There was something beautiful about him all the time, but the shapes and contours of his body were a work of art. Naked and smiling, he knelt in front of the sofa and unfastened the button of her jeans then let his hands drag over her skin as he used his thumbs and the palms of his hands to slide them down until she could pull her feet out.

At the gentlest urging, she twisted to sit up and threw her head back at the first lick, cried out when his mouth moved over her clit and he slid a finger inside her. Normally, Fiona loved all the foreplay, but she wanted him inside her.

She sat forward. "Please, now."

With a hand on her chest, he pushed her back and continued licking and sucking until her heart pounded and every breath came attached to a moan. The pressure built, and she probably would have died if he'd stopped. His moan vibrated against her clit, and she fell over the edge. Her body writhed and every inch, every cell in her body caught fire. She cried out a final time and collapsed against the back of the couch. She needed a minute to slow her heart. But just one.

Grier smiled as she tugged him up then down on top of her. "Oh, God, Fiona." He moved with an urgency she needed. But oh, God, she wanted more.

He drove into her over and over, and her hips rose to meet him, her legs wrapped around him, and her hands urged him deeper, harder, faster. Need powered through her.

Every thrust brought her closer until finally, the waves of her passion crested, and her body blew apart. Grier tensed and shuddered then collapsed onto his elbows.

"Let's go home."

* * *

GRIER HELD Fiona's hand as they walked from his bike up to the porch. She stopped on the second step and pulled him back when he continued. "Grier."

The front door stood open, not far but enough, and the wood at the latch plate was splintered. Shit. Again.

He reached for the gun he'd taken to carrying at his

back, checked the clip, then slid the bolt. Sedotal or not, someone wasn't walking out of their house.

He shielded Fiona and walked ahead, gun against his thigh out of sight of whatever lurked inside the broken door. He pushed it open and peeked inside.

"Don't be shy, big brother. Come in." He motioned with his gun to Grier, who slipped his own pistol to Fiona then shoved her back. Sedotal waved him in again.

"How dare you come into my home!" Grier shouted at Tyler.

Grier held up his hands and walked in, Fiona behind him. This woman had no sense of danger. She busted in, gun hand extended and started firing at Tyler's men. The Omens weren't prepared for this kind of an attack coming from Fiona and it wasn't long before Fiona had taken all the men out and it was just Tyler left standing.

"You have no idea how long I've wanted to do that," Fiona smirked.

"Let me!" Grier said as Fiona pointed her weapon in Tyler's direction.

"It's time for us to fight like real brothers." Grier lowered his weapon as Tyler laughed and followed suit. They started circling each other, neither of them going for the first hit. Grier smiled back at Tyler as Fiona watched on, witnessing something she never thought she'd have to.

"You don't understand who I am..." Grier began just as Tyler swung his arm and hit Grier on the chin. Fiona gasped but didn't do anything; she stood still, a mere observer. She knew Grier could handle it and just like that Grier was on top of Tyler, his hands around his neck while he pressed his legs to Tyler's arms, giving him no chance of fighting back. Grier was strong, Fiona knew that and she could only imagine the power of his body weight pressing down on Tyler's lungs, making it harder for him to breathe. Tyler was completely and utterly helpless beneath Grier. Fiona could sense the fear radiating off him as he realized he was no match.

Fiona watched as Tyler began to lose any real fight left in him, he slowly stopped struggling and started clawing at Grier's hands around his neck, clearly trying to beg for air. But Grier didn't care. He looked Tyler dead in the eyes and said, "You should've never laid your dirty hands on my wife! Ever!"

Then using all of his strength Grier tightened his hands even more around Tyler's neck and finally, he was almost out. Fiona had seen a lot of fights over the last two years, but she had never witnessed someone killing with their bare hands.

"Now let me finish him", Fiona reached forward and pointed her gun at Tyler.

"Fucking... bitch," Tyler said weakly and breathlessly.

Fiona smiled, enjoying his fear and fired right into his skull.

Grier looked around and saw all the men laying in bloody heaps on the floor. It looked like a war zone. There were bullet holes all over the living room where it had all gone down, most of the furniture had been destroyed.

"I'll call our guys to come clear this up," he told Fiona who hadn't moved much since she had shot Tyler.

"Okay, good. We'll need some cash to pay off the cops, we can't have this getting out," she said as she came back from deep, contemplative thoughts. "We'll need to get the news out that Tyler and his men are dead. They need to know they should not cross us again, especially now that Tyler has been taken out once and for all."

"Get some rest Fi, I'm on it," Grier said softly as he kissed Fiona on the forehead.

19

It was after three in the morning before the police let her go with strict instructions that she shouldn't leave town. Which was fine because Kye was already on his way to bring London home. And Fiona couldn't wait.

"Are you okay?" Grier held her hand as the cab brought them back to the clubhouse.

Okay? She'd shot a man. But he was the kind of man the world was better off without, so there was that. And she was… okay enough.

"Yeah." She nodded and stared out of the window. She would be much better when she had her baby back. Hopefully, soon.

Things had been so unsettled since… she couldn't remember a time they had ever been settled, at least not since she married Grier. And now that she didn't have

Sedotal and the Omens to worry about, she felt lighter, more in control of her emotions.

"I'm afraid we're going to turn into one of those old married couples." She smiled at him for no other reason than she felt like smiling. And afraid wasn't the right word. Hoping was definitely more accurate.

Grier grinned. And God she loved that grin. "As long as old married couples have a lot of sex, I'm okay with things being more normal."

The cab driver chuckled, covered his mouth, and looked at Fiona in the mirror. "Sorry." He continued. "My experience with being an old married guy is that the sex isn't what could be described as 'a lot.'"

Fiona shot him a wink. "I'm not worried." She twisted just enough to drop her free hand into Grier's lap and gave a little squeeze.

"I think we're gonna be okay, too," Grier leaned in for a kiss.

The driver turned down Hell Hollow road and bumped along until they pulled up in front of the club-house. Grier paid him then helped Fiona out of the car. She wanted him. For the rest of her life she would want him, but her need was urgent. The adrenaline from everything that had happened was starting to die away and peace settled over her. She just wanted him. Not for any other reason than she loved him more than she'd ever thought would happen for them. Before they walked inside, she stopped and turned. When his arms came around her, she knew there was no better place, no Mayberry she would love more than the one they'd created for themselves.

He kissed her forehead, her nose, then brushed his mouth over hers. This was where she belonged.

They walked inside, and Fiona looked around. This was home. Her legacy. The bar, the office she'd given her own special flair, the friends who came forward to welcome them back and hear the story. Max might have "gifted" her this job, but she'd earned the right to keep it.

It took hours. She'd told the story a hundred times, listened to Grier tell it a hundred more, but finally, they were alone in the room she'd claimed as hers a long time before she took over for Max. It was the place she stayed when she was scared, because knowing Hamilton was only a few rooms over made her feel secure.

She slipped out of her jeans and shirt then settled next to him on the bed. "This is nice." She wasn't talking about the room—it was okay, but not special—or the bed or the new blankets. She meant lying next to her freshly showered husband with his arms around her, his body pressed against hers.

"Better than nice." His voice, low and sweet, sent ripples of pleasure through her. So much about him made her heart pitter-patter, but his voice warmed her almost as much as the hand stroking her arm.

She let her fingers drift over his stomach down to the towel at his waist, as she shifted to drag her lips across his chest then his throat, his chin, and his mouth. He tasted like warm whiskey and oranges, felt like her own slice of heaven.

She curled her fingers around his cock and smiled at his groan. "I think you saved my life today."

"You saved mine first." He ran his thumb over her mouth and smiled when she nipped at it. "Not just today. Way back in Belize when you showed up all dangerous and threatening my life."

"Thought you liked it there." She could barely think at all because he'd quit talking and started swirling his tongue over her nipple.

"Like it here better." He pushed her onto her back and slid down her body. When he lifted her leg and laid it over his back, he looked up and grinned. "But this is my favorite."

Oh, dear God. Her muscles tightened and coiled as he worked his tongue over her, and her body burned. He brought her to the edge then pulled back, teasing until she cried out and wiggled, using her legs to try to bring him back. "Please, don't stop."

"Don't stop what?" She tried to raise up, to push his head back down, but he put his hand on her shoulder. "Be still." He grazed his hand over her clit, and she cried out. "What do you want, Fiona?"

His voice purred through her. "Lick me." He ran his tongue over her thigh. "Lick my pussy."

And he did until she was writhing, the pressure so intense she couldn't hold back. Her body exploded, and she gripped the blanket trying to anchor herself.

Fiona wanted more, wanted his dick inside her, his weight on top of her. She scraped her nails over his shoulder. "Now, Grier. Fuck me." Her blood burned and her eyes fluttered shut.

He lifted himself over her, moved his hips to let his cock swipe over her, and she gasped. Oh, God. Oh, God. Oh, God. There was something magical about this man and that cock. And when he pushed inside her, she clung to him, clenched her muscles around him, smiled when he blew out a breath. Fair was fair and if he was going to try to make her heart explode, she could fight back a little.

He moved slowly, his gaze locked onto hers, and she pulled him down for a kiss that seared her inside and out. Every thrust drove her higher, building the passion, making her body tremble until again, she blew apart. This time she held onto him as he shuddered and groaned.

"If this is being one of those old married couples," he kissed her forehead, "sign me up."

"Oh yeah, me too."

He rolled away but gathered her closer so she could

lay her head on his chest. The steady beat of his heart lulled her, and if she never felt another moment of happiness, this one would see her through to the end of her life. "I love you." His whispered words accompanied a kiss to the top of her head.

"I love you, too." She gazed up at him. "You know, we have a day or so before Kye brings London home. I feel like we should make the most of it." And all it took was one kiss to convince him.

GRIER KNOCKED on the bathroom door. They still had a truck to unload, beds to set up, and pizza to order. And since she'd left him in charge of moving their stuff into their new house, one with a white picket fence lined by rose bushes, and a big backyard, he was taking care of his chores in the order of their importance. "What do you want on the pizza?" She didn't answer, so he knocked again. "Fiona."

"Grier, go away. I'm busy in here peeing on a stick."

What? "Why are you peeing on a stick?" He'd heard of a lot of things, peeing on trees, in the woods, on the side of the road, but that was guys mostly, and not something he could see Fiona doing.

She flung open the door and waved the stick in question. "Because my period is late."

"Oh." Then… "Oh! Are you?"

Technology these days made the answer so fast. She flipped the test around to look at the little window. It felt as if it took hours for her to answer. Finally, she nodded.

"We're…?" Another baby? He hadn't completely adapted to the first one yet. She nodded again and waited. "Wow." Not that they'd practiced much in the way of safe sex. "Another baby."

London had just started walking, babbling Mama, and feeding herself, which always led to an inevitable mess. And now there would be two messes. Two babies. Two car seats. Two everything. Holy shit.

She must have seen his panic. "Are you okay?"

"Can we handle two?" He did okay with London, but that was because Fiona was usually nearby. "I mean, two is a lot."

She twisted her mouth to one side. "I think it's a little late to worry now." There was that. "Besides, we've managed so far." She moved closer, her hand on his shoulder. "Think of it as an adventure."

An adventure. Yeah. But infinitely scarier than rock climbing or riding his motorcycle without a helmet. He nodded quietly, still picturing the horrors of fatherhood to two. "An adventure."

"Yeah, like waking up every morning and not knowing what joy the day's going to bring." Her smile stretched across her face and her eyes sparkled. And that was enough to make Grier happy. Scared still, but happy. She smiled. "It's gonna be two times as great."

He pulled her in close, inhaled the scent of her hair, kissed the top of her head. "It definitely is."

"It's good news, right?"

They'd been through so much over the last few months with Grier finding out the identity of his parents, with losing Jez and Hamilton, with Fiona killing Sedotal, that this good news seemed almost odd to hear and Grier wasn't sure if he could let himself hope. But for Fiona, there was nothing he wouldn't do, and if she was happy, he was happy. She was back where she belonged, running her father's business, making a life with Grier and London and now a new baby. They'd bought a new house and left all the ugliness of the past behind. "You bet."

20

They'd only been on the road for a few hours, but Sage pulled the bike into a motel some-where on the Georgia coast. Mia lifted her head and untangled her arms from around him. Since Fiona had rescued her, she hadn't quite been herself. Certainly, the bullet wound, a through and through just above her hip bone, couldn't have been comfortable so he understood.

"I'll get us a room." His voice was gruff, deeper than he'd ever heard himself speak. But having her head against his back, her arms around his waist, her legs alongside his ass, for the last four hours had affected him in ways he didn't like to think about.

It had been years since he'd... been with anyone, even though he'd let everyone at the Demon clubhouse think he was working his way through the Hell Kats and the Wall Kats, he'd not touched anyone. Couldn't. Not that he didn't want to, but… his mind and his body weren't exactly on speaking terms.

He walked into the motel office and plunked down a couple of hundred-dollar bills. The kid at the counter eyed them and Grier unwrapped another but held it in his hand. "I need a room."

The kid behind the counter couldn't have been more than a high schooler. His acne hadn't cleared up and his glasses were held together with a piece of tape at the corner where the left lens met the earwand. The kid put his comic down and eyed the money. "We don't take cash. Only credit cards."

Sage peeled another hundred and put both on the counter on top of the others. "Look, kid, I need an empty room for one night. You don't even have to put it on the books. Just take the money and give me a key and the number of a pizza place that delivers."

The kid looked left then right then at Sage. He slid a key across the counter. "Room six is open and clean." He smiled. "Ice machine's broken and there's a condom machine bolted in each bathroom. Takes ones and fives."

Condom machine? He looked at the sign over the kid's shoulder. It showed nightly rates and below it, ones for hourly rental. The condom machine made more sense now. Sage took a copy of the takeout menu the kid handed him and walked out to the bike. He nodded to Mia. "Room six."

Mia stretched her back then winced. "Feels like I have a white-hot poker in my side and a bike seat fused to my ass." She chuckled and held the spot where she'd been shot. "I'm not sure which is worse."

He tried not to look at the aforementioned ass as she walked in front of him, but this woman had a body that would make the most chaste of priests stand for a good gawk. And Sage Anderson might have been chaste of late, but he was certainly no priest. No sir. He was a Screaming Demon, a former Marine gunnery sergeant, a tech wizard. Priest didn't make the list. As a matter of fact, churches probably groaned in relief when he passed on by and didn't stop for a chat. Not that he didn't try to be good. Sometimes, life just got in the way of his intentions.

It didn't matter much now anyway. He'd gone to the dark side a while ago and there wasn't much chance he would go back.

He focused, walking around Mia to unlock the door. He pushed it open and let her walk ahead of him. The room wasn't bad. Two beds. A table. A TV and a bathroom. Not the worst place he'd ever put his head down and better than Afghanistan by at least about a hundred degrees. Not quite as good as the Demon clubhouse after Fiona renovated it, but it would do long enough for Mia to rest her injury.

Her breath came in short puffs as she lifted the hem

of her shirt to check her bandage. He had more in his bag on the bike. "I'll be right back." He needed a minute anyway now that he'd seen all that smooth olive skin across her belly. Need stirred in his gut and he stopped walking. What the hell? He hadn't been so… turned on in years. Not since…

Nope. Not going there. Not now. The last thing he needed was to start bawling in the middle of a skeezy motel parking lot. He walked to the bike, flipped open the lid to the bag and pulled out the bandages and tape he'd brought along with them. By the time he got back to the room, she'd removed the old bandage and stood at the sink in the bathroom turning a formerly almost white washcloth a light shade of pink. "Still bleeding?" Maybe he should take her to the hospital.

She jumped. "Just seeping a little, I think. Can you wash the one in the back? It hurts when I twist to try." A fine sheen of sweat covered her skin.

"Are you okay?" He took the cloth and held it while she turned and lifted the back of her shirt.

Oh, God help him. More smooth skin. More than he needed to see in his current state of distress. And by distress he meant arousal.

"Yeah. It just hurts a little when I move. Maybe I should just get a ride to my folks' house in…" She stuttered and stammered. "Atlanta."

Any idiot could have seen that she was lying. "I could rent a car."

She pulled her lower lip between her teeth and the tip of her tongue peeked out to moisten it. "Maybe if I rest, we can try riding again tomorrow."

"Mia." Rest wasn't enough. She needed a doctor.

"Sage, if I go to the hospital, they'll report the gunshot. And for reasons I would rather not discuss, I don't need my name to show up on a police report, okay?" Tears slipped down her cheek and her lip quivered. "Please?"

He nodded and gently ran the washcloth over the wound then applied the ointment that Fiona had given him before they left. At his touch, she sucked in a breath and he drew back. "Did I hurt you?"

She shook her head and looked at him in the mirror over the sink. "No." Her skin flushed, and he took the bandage she'd opened from her hand.

Touching her was like running his fingertips over satin. And his body responded. Dammit. He drew back. "Okay."

When he didn't move right away, she looked over her shoulder. "Sage?"

Shit. He still needed to tape the bandage in place. "Right." And that his hand was shaking didn't mean a damned thing. Not one. It meant he was nervous, meant he didn't want to hurt her. It meant... nothing he would admit to or that a quick adjustment of his jeans wouldn't hide.

He pushed the tape down and ran his finger along the edge to seal it to her skin, careful to touch only the tape.

Goddammit. What was it with this woman? She'd been a thorn in his side since the first minute he'd met her. Since she'd first walked into the clubhouse behind Jez and he'd gotten a look at all that long black hair and those chocolatey brown eyes, the curve of her ass, and that spot in the small of her back where he imagined resting his hand when he imagined kissing her. And he had. Too many times to count and way too many times for this to be a comfortable moment.

She lowered her shirt and turned. Oh, for hell's sake. How hadn't he ever noticed the flecks of amber and gold in her eyes? The streaks of lighter brown in her coal-black hair. And noticing now wasn't helping his situation.

She tilted her chin up and her lips parted. Oh, God. He'd seen desire before, knew what it looked like. And he wanted to kiss her, wanted to hear her moan his name.

Stop. This had to stop. He couldn't keep thinking about her this way. He was her protector, the man who would save her from harm, no matter what it took.

But those doe eyes... luscious lips... oh, God. He

lowered his head, just for one taste. But she wrapped her arms around his neck, caressed the back of his head where he kept the hair military short. And she whimpered in his mouth as she pushed her body against his and angled her head to deepen the kiss. He couldn't have stopped kissing her if a meteor crashed into the earth and he was the man charged with saving it.

He tried to pull away, or thought he should, but instead he lifted her and set her on the sink, cupping his hands under her ass and moaning at the feel. Jesus. He needed to stop. Stop kissing her. Stop touching her. Stop wanting her.

Damned if he knew how. Not with her lips touching his, her tongue in his mouth. Hell, if he could have, he would have stayed right there for the rest of his life. She was intoxicating. Magical.

Shit. Sage Anderson was in trouble. Deep. Trouble.

MIA KISSED him as if her life depended on it. He was everything she'd imagined him to be and so much more. Under her hands, she could feel the corded muscles in his chest and back, and he had an ass like a cantaloupe, firm, round and thoroughly biteable, if a girl was into that kind of thing.

There were three things Giovanni women liked -

garlic in… everything, short tight skirts with stiletto heels that could kill a man if necessary, and men with firm, round asses. Although she'd never quite felt like a true Giovanni woman, not since she was about seven, but she knew the family traits and also knew when she had them.

Not only was he a handsome devil, but he kissed like one, too. And that alone made her panties almost dissolve. But she couldn't let herself go, not with him. She'd broken one rule for him already. Let him kiss her on the mouth. She'd caught the idea of making such a rule from a movie, but it worked. It kept what she'd done as a Demon Wall Kat then Hell Kat separate from the person she was. What she did to survive was one thing, letting herself fall into a trap because of it was another.

She had enough sense to know the difference and the importance of separation of powers. And by God, she'd keep her rules. After this. As soon as she was done kissing him. But he pulled back before she had the chance. Before she was ready, if she was honest. Instead, she put a hand against her chest and tried to quiet its rabid throbbing.

He leaned against the wall behind him and scrubbed his hands over his face. "God, I'm so sorry. I don't know what came over me."

"It bothers you, right?' She'd known. All along, she'd

known being a Kat at the clubhouse would mean no man would want her. She was too used, too damaged. And she had more baggage than Samsonite.

"What?"

"Never mind." She flung the bathroom door open and stomped to the bed nearest the front window. She threw back the blankets and crawled between the sheets.

He walked out slowly, his brows drawn together and his mouth almost puckered. He stood at the edge of her bed, and she concentrated on his knees which were directly in her line of sight. "Please. Mia, tell me what you're talking about."

She sat up and pushed the sheet to her lap. "It's none of your business." Her side ached when she fell back against the mattress.

"It is my business. It's about me. Me kissing you."

"Why'd you stop?" It wasn't just a question. It was a challenge. And if he answered, maybe she would, too but not one damned minute before.

"Because."

She turned away, faced the window, and ignored him.

"Mia… please." He sighed and she heard his hands scrub over the stubble on his cheeks. "Shit. Fine. I stopped because I can't want you this much and still be able to keep you safe."

"Keep me safe?" Bull shit.

"Now you. What did you mean? What do you think bothers me?" His eyes narrowed and he shoved his hands in his pockets.

Why, oh why, did he have to look so adorable? "That I was a Kat for the club. It's okay. I know it's bad. I'm not the kind of girl any guy would ever... I'm not..." Fuck. Why did this have to be so hard? And why did she care if he didn't think she was marriage material. "Not the kind of girl you bring home to meet your mom. Or the kind you picture having babies with." And now she sounded like she was lobbying for a marriage proposal. Could this get worse? "Not that I want to have your babies or anything."

He frowned. "What's wrong with my babies?"

What? "Nothing, I'm sure. They'll be beautiful and very... tall. But they'll just be with someone else." Well, yes, as a matter of fact, she could make it worse. And had. "Not that I care. I mean... your babies are your business. And whoever you have them with." She sighed. "God make it stop."

"Make what stop?" But his lips twitched.

"The babbling." She fiddled with the blanket where it rested over her chest. "I do it when I'm nervous." And now she'd admitted he made her nervous. Perfect.

"Nervous, huh?" He looked down at his shoes and rocked back on his heels. "Me, too." After a second of silence that felt like a solid month, he nodded to the door. "I'm going to go outside and call Grier. Check in. You gonna be okay for a few minutes? I'll be right outside."

She nodded because she was too ashamed to speak. She'd humiliated herself too many times to count tonight. And it wasn't until she closed her eyes that it occurred to her that he hadn't denied that her past as a Kat bothered him. And pretending not to cry while she pretended to sleep was a lot harder than it sounded.

DARK DESIRES

~ A billionaire dark romance series ~

Dark Desire

Dark Rules

Dark Secret

Dark Time

Dark Truth

BARRE TO BAR

~ A billionaire second chance series ~

Dancing With Lies

Dancing With Temptation

Dancing With Doubt

Dancing With Guilt

Dancing With Redemption

TWISTED INTENTION
~ A billionaire revenge romance series ~
Twisted Beauty
Twisted Love
Twisted Fate

Mafia's Obsession
~ A hot mafia romance series ~
Mafia's Dirty Secret
Mafia's Fake Bride
Mafia's Final Play

Screaming Demons
~ An MC romance series full of suspense ~
Rough Start
Rough Ride
Rough Choice
Rough Patch
Rough Return
Rough Road
Rough Trip
Rough Night
Rough Love

Standalone Contemporary Romance
Billionaire in Vegas
Billionaire Hunt

Billionaire's Game

Billionaire Retreat

Billionaire On Air

A Chance To Love

Somebody To Love

Not Mine To Love

Check out Summer's entire collection at
www.summercooper.com/books

ABOUT SUMMER COOPER

Thank you so much for reading. Without you, it wouldn't be possible for me to be a full-time author. I hope you enjoy reading my books as much as I do writing them.

Besides (obviously!) reading and writing, I also love cuddling my dogs, shouting at Alexa, being upside down (aka Yoga) and driving my family cray-cray!

Get in touch at
hello@summercooper.com
www.summercooper.com

facebook.com/summercooperauthor
instagram.com/summercooperauthor
goodreads.com/summercooper
bookbub.com/profile/summer-cooper